sure as sugar

and other stories

Camille Hernández-Ramdwar

RARE
MACHINES

Publisher: Kwame Scott Fraser | Acquiring editor: Julie Mannell
Cover designer: Laura Boyle
Cover image: Saccharum officinarum Blanco by Francisco Manuel Blanco, 1880; Hummingbird: Brockhaus' Konversations-Lexikon by Leipzig G. Mützel, 1892

Library and Archives Canada Cataloguing in Publication

Title: Suite as sugar : and other stories / Camille Hernández-Ramdwar.
Names: Hernández-Ramdwar, Camille, 1965- author.
Identifiers: Canadiana (print) 20220398003 | Canadiana (ebook) 20220398011 | ISBN 9781459750715 (softcover) | ISBN 9781459750722 (PDF) | ISBN 9781459750739 (EPUB)
Classification: LCC PS8615.E7535 S85 2023 | DDC C813/.6—dc23

  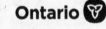 

We acknowledge the support of the Canada Council for the Arts and the Ontario Arts Council for our publishing program. We also acknowledge the financial support of the Government of Ontario, through the Ontario Book Publishing Tax Credit and Ontario Creates, and the Government of Canada.

Care has been taken to trace the ownership of copyright material used in this book. The author and the publisher welcome any information enabling them to rectify any references or credits in subsequent editions.

The publisher is not responsible for websites or their content unless they are owned by the publisher.

Printed and bound in Canada.

Rare Machines, an imprint of Dundurn Press
1382 Queen Street East
Toronto, Ontario, Canada M4L 1C9
dundurn.com, @dundurnpress 𝕏 f ⊙

suite as sugar

To J.
So many stories.

Contents

It's Lit

We started off many moons ago, long before these glass-and-steel towers were here. A certain mayor who was like *noooooooooobody!* (well, before *another* mayor came on the scene who was an even bigger joke, with his crack-smoking, bumboclaat self) wanted to oust us from where we had established settlement. We weren't doing anything different than what others before us had done — the Anishinaabek, and then after them, the stink-foot British soldiers, building their bleddy Fort York. When the bulldozers came in that day and forced us out, the contractors handing us little pink slips of paper as if we had been fired from our homes, it raised something up in me. I remember people were crying, women were screaming; one man was on the toilet when they came. They gave us ten minutes to clear out. Ten minutes to pack up our lives. I was only fifteen at the time, but I looked older, so nobody was the wiser, and therefore no one confiscated me like some contraband and carted me off to a group or foster home or any of those death traps. From there, we skirted the perimeter of the city for a while until things calmed down. Meanwhile, all the fancy condos came into being. Sentinel after sentinel after sentinel, thirty, forty storeys high, towering over Lake Ontario, the Gardiner Expressway, the CN railway track. People staring into each other's homes day and night, each building topped with cherry lights to prevent the planes landing at Billy Bishop Airport from crashing into them in the fog or a snowstorm. So many homes, thousands and thousands — and nothing for us. We came back bit by bit; we infiltrated and set up shop under the Gardiner Expressway. So now all these condo-dwellers had something to watch, something to report on Facebook and Twitter, something to laugh about and mock, something to call the cops about. They were busy on their devices, surveilling us and, whenever they could, trying to get us evicted from our new settlements. The thing that seemed to set them off most was the fires. As if that was *any* danger to them! No, me and my buddies could see all our gear go up in flames because some meth head lost his damn mind, or because somebody had beef with someone else and outta spite threw a match. But these rich idiots were actually scared that somehow a fire under a concrete ramp was gonna reach up to their forty-second-storey, seven-hundred-thousand-dollar condo and burn them alive. Either that or the smoke was "annoying" to them. Holy fuck.

It was around this time that I heard a lot of these condo units were just sitting empty. That really bugged me. Especially in January and February, the hardest months in Toronto, when you were moving from place to place, freezing your ass off, sometimes risking a shelter for a day or two, sometimes riding the subway or just trying to stay underground in the PATH, the spiderweb of corridors linking the big, expensive office buildings with the big, expensive condo buildings and the subway systems and the subterranean shopping malls. The PATH is supposedly the biggest underground shopping mall in the world. You could get lost in there for a while, but eventually some disgruntled security guard would come for you and tell you to move along, and if you didn't, they would call the cops. Sometimes you could go into a public library and try to catch a few Zs or, with a few loonies begged, go sit in the Tim Hortons, nursing a double-double. Anything to stay outta the cold and stay alive. I could never do what a lot of us folks do: sleep on those subway grates on King Street and other high-falutin' places where the stockbrokers and bankers and other money-managing people worked. I used to watch these fools when riding the King streetcar, watch the way they would gingerly step around a sleeping human burrito strewn haphazardly over a steaming subway grate, careful that their Michael Kors boots didn't make any contact, that their camel-hair coats and Harry Rosen suits remained pristine and uncontaminated by this hominid detritus.

So, sitting in the underground PATH one day, my sneakers wet from having traversed a few blocks of soggy, dirty, slushy snow, I picked up a discarded *Globe and Mail* and found an article about these so-called ghost hotels. The author estimated that sixty-five hundred homes in Toronto were being rented out on sites like Airbnb, so people couldn't actually live in them, and that kept rents extremely high for everyone else. Well, completely out of reach for people like me is more like it! Even if ten of us grouped together, we still wouldn't be able to afford to live in one of these fancy-ass buildings. I was pissed! The article continued, talking about some guy who, with his mom, had amassed a couple of apartment buildings, kicked the tenants out, and just started raking in Airbnb dough. Where he got the millions to do this? The guy was like twenty-six years old! Younger than me! What the fuck.

The truth was, our numbers were growing. If people thought Toronto had a homeless problem before, when Mike Harris was in power in the nineties, what they were seeing now was a hundred times worse. I mean, it used to only be people who had mental problems, damaged youths escaping foster homes and abusive living arrangements, drug addicts. But now, more and more, I was seeing plain ordinary folks, like single moms and their children, and recently arrived immigrants who could barely speak English and just couldn't afford rent anywhere but had to stay in the city to access services. There were also refugees who were either awaiting a hearing or had been denied their claim to stay in Canada and were on the lam. This meant things got a lot more colourful too! I mean, I was always one of the ones on the fringe, with my Anishinaabek eyes and my frizzy hair (never mind my dress and my, uh, ambiguous appearance. I mean, I know people were always trying to figure out if I was a boy or a girl, and I liked to keep 'em guessing). But, damn, there were a lot of coloured people suddenly joining our ranks. Kinda made it easier for me in some ways, but also drew more attention to us on the whole, 'cause racist cops, being who they are, now had another reason to come at us — with brute force too.

So between the very privileged NIMBY folks living in Liberty Village and CityPlace and along the Waterfront, and the sweltering summer months which laid us bare for all to see (on the real: some of my cohort took to sunbathing naked like hippies at Woodstock, even skinny-dipping in Lake Ontario), and our increasing and encroaching presence in these ungated communities, the City decided it need to open some kind of human warehousing before the cruelty of winter was upon us. Enter the respite centres. What a name! I wondered if these Prada-wearing, Audi-driving NIMBYs would have gone for a "respite" in one of them, away from their jacuzzied terraces and Olympic-size swimming pools. The City erected a giant canvas dome meant to house a hundred of us, but of course by the time the frost was nipping in November, we were nearly triple that number.

One night I was trying to stay warm in a tiny plexiglass shelter that was owned by a boat tour company. With no boat tours in the cold months, we took it over. It was right down by the lake. Normally, this would be a terrible place to seek shelter, as the winds whipping off Lake Ontario could paralyze you, but tonight was relatively mild for fall. Jack, the legless guy who actually lived there year-round, had opened up a can of ravioli and was eating it with a spork. I was drinking some Jägermeister I had acquired from a buddy earlier in the day. Teisha was there with her son; he had fallen asleep in his stroller and she had covered him up with an old coat. Magan, our newest cohort member, was also there, staring off into space again. I felt for Magan. I knew he was anxiously anticipating what this winter would bring. This would be his third in Canada. His first one, he nearly died waiting for a bus. Waited and waited, and like the bus wasn't coming, or I don't know what. Maybe it was delayed because of the snow. And that day Magan was wearing only a thin coat and track pants and some canvas sneakers — no hat, no gloves. He didn't know about dressing for winter, coming from Somalia. He had a kind of nervous breakdown waiting there for the bus that never came, his hands and feet getting numb, not understanding that he was slowly freezing to death, and he collapsed in a snowbank. Somebody saw him there, through their living room window, and called an ambulance to come and cart him off to emerg.

It was Teisha who first told us about the Movement. Her child father was working as a concierge in one of the older, well-heeled condos right on the Waterfront, and he had heard from a buddy of his that momentum was building, but everyone was kinda paranoid, so Teisha told us we had to be real on the down low about it all. Not only had word spread about all the ghost units in the hundreds of condo buildings running along Queens Quay

West, through CityPlace, the Waterfront, Fort York, and Liberty Village — all our stomping grounds — but plans were brewing for some kind of dramatic action, a massive intervention. As it would take more than homeless people to pull this off, others were also involved. The cleaners who worked in these buildings had joined the Movement. God knows they had it rough having to clean up Sunday morning vomit in stairwells on the regular and constant French Bulldog piss and shit every damn day inside the swanky elevators, in addition to picking up endless cigarette butts that these freakin' affluent pigs flung — lit — off their balconies, causing endless balcony fires. (And they complained about us? *Us?*) Most cleaning staff didn't speak English well, and this was often their first job in Canada. But still they were down. Concierge and security staff were definitely in. They had also taken so much crap from these richy riches that they were only too happy to oblige an invasion of the luxurious retreats they worked in by the likes of us. Many had even been in our shoes, had spent a night or two in a shelter or on the street, because like the cleaners, most were recent immigrants who could not speak English too well yet and were being endlessly harassed by Kondo Kunt Karen and Investment Property Prick Peter, shouted at, abused, blamed for things well beyond their control. Teisha told us that on more than one occasion, her child father had had his life threatened.

As Teisha talked, I looked up at the many towers in my vista. I started to count how many blacked-out windows I saw — no lights on, although it was 8:00 p.m. I figured if someone could log these windows night after night, we could eventually figure out which condos were typically uninhabited. If we combined this information with intel from the concierges, we could get a good estimate of how many units to hit. I told Teisha about my plan.

"Well, you should come to the next meeting" was all she said.

And so I was recruited by the Movement. I got myself a cheap notebook from the dollar store and a pen, and every night I would walk around the neighbourhoods, keeping track of every blacked-out window that stayed black from sundown to sun-up. Sometimes this meant I had to get up in the middle of the night and check, but I didn't mind. I had always had trouble sleeping from childhood, so this was some distraction from the nightmares that frequently plagued me. Someone suggested that instead of me having to keep notes, we should really be taking pictures of the buildings and marking out the windows on some kind of graph. I was like, *yeah, take pictures with what?* But at the next meeting we were all handed brand-new iPhones and Samsungs and Huaweis — high-end shit.

When I turned mine on, a picture of a Chinese lady popped up as the profile pic. I realized this was her phone. "What about tracking?" I shouted, afraid now that some cops would find our secret meeting place and buss down the door and cart us off to jail.

But Rex told me, "Nah worry, my lord. We done deal wid *dat* star!" Rex was one of the main organizers, and it seemed like nothing really perturbed him at all.

So weeks passed and we continued to monitor the buildings and the windows, and at our meetings everything was being mapped out on a graph so we could organize and strategize how this would all go down. The number of recruits was growing as well. I knew, too, that I was only seeing the people who were showing up for meetings, and behind each of them were many more — the ones they were looking out for: partners, children, family, friends.

Then all hell broke loose.

The Christmas season had begun. Snow had already fallen a few times, and all along Queens Quay they put up the same damn Christmas decorations on the street lamps they did every year: angels and stars and evergreen branches and musical notes by the Music Garden and whatever. The condo buildings glittered and twinkled as many balconies were now strung with all manner of Christmas lights: flashing, multicoloured, blinking, fading in and out, purple, white, red, green, yellow, large, small, differently shaped. In the midst of all this merriment, the government decided to announce new legislation that eliminated rent control. Additionally, they increased public transit fares and made massive cuts to student funding. Some of the respite centres were to be closed thanks to the constant complaints from the NIMBY committees that had sprung up in each neighbourhood. Friends of mine told me that some of the services they accessed — that even *I* accessed — were being cut or "disappeared": services for trans youth, Aboriginal family services, services for survivors of domestic abuse, post-incarceration services, mental health walk-in clinics, needle exchange programs ... The list was long. The media responded by calling it the Grinch Budget, but because these cuts really affected us — the homeless, the downtrodden, the "sufferahs," as Rex would say — I just felt that on the whole Toronto did not care what happened. They probably hoped we would all take a long walk off a short pier right into frigid Lake Ontario, and then they could enjoy their condo enclaves and bespoke bars and restaurants and their coconut milk cascara lattes in peace.

After that budget announcement, the Movement ramped up. Winter would soon be fully upon us, and we knew that there would be more and more people in need of real shelter. Time was of the essence. We chose a date of action: December 4.

We organized into cells. Each cell was responsible for occupying a building. We had coordinated with our concierge members and cleaning staff to make sure at least one of each of them were on duty during the occupation. Pass-keys for each building had been copied and distributed.

The plan was to set off the fire alarms in each and every building from Queens Quay and York Street to the western edge of Liberty Village. Once alarms were activated, we were to text the code words to our HQ: *IT'S LIT.*

In the ensuing chaos, as EMS and police would be trying to figure out exactly what the hell was going on, we would wait until most of the condo residents had evacuated, and then we would use the stairs in each building to find our vacant units, use our pass-keys to enter, and then unfurl banners from the balconies, claim-ing occupancy. The majority of these were flags with a simple fire emoji blown up on them (as in *Light It Up!*). Others said *Affordable Housing for All!!*, *People Not Profit*, and *The Fire Next Time*. Our intent was to occupy as many vacant units as possible with as many people as we could find, and then simply stay lodged as long as we could to make our point. If we won, fine; if we didn't, at least we would not be spending another Christmas on the streets.

December 4 came. The Action was planned for 6:00 p.m. Hoping not to draw too much attention to the sight of hundreds of homeless people amassing, we did our best to disperse in local coffee shops and convenience stores and other sites in proximity to the targeted buildings. I was at the Circle K convenience store at Bathurst and Lake Shore. The teams were targeting three build-ings nearby: the Waverley, the Rosewood, and the Bonne Chance. Some of my team members were in the Circle K with me, while others were farther up Bathurst Street at the Tim's. Another group was sheltering in the nearby community centre. We had timed everything — the minutes it would take to walk to each building and the estimated time it would take for us to reach our units on each floor.

At six on the dot our phones all beeped and buzzed at the same time. Same message: *IT'S LIT.*

There were nine of us: me, Pooky and her girlfriend Jeans, Chantel from Quebec, Jeremy (who had a prosthetic leg), Magan and his cousin who had recently arrived from Somalia, and Shree and her teenage daughter. I remember rushing through that cold night to the back entrance of the Bonne Chance and waiting by one of the stairwell exit doors. It flung open and some residents came out looking pissed, no jackets on, bitching about the alarm. I grabbed the door and we all pushed inside, daring anyone to say anything, but the residents were too busy complaining to notice, so we began our trek. Sixth, twelfth, and nineteenth floors. It had already been predetermined that Jeremy and Shree and her daughter would occupy the closest unit since they might have the hardest time with the stairs, while the rest of us would keep ascending.

I was headed to the nineteenth floor with Pooky and Jeans. I don't think I had ever run up so many flights of stairs so fast in my life. Especially after we'd dropped off the rest of the gang at their respective floors, we just busted it to get to our destination.

Unit 1903. Here we were. I pushed the pass-key into the lock and turned it. The door swung open.

We couldn't believe our eyes. This was one of the Airbnb condos, and it had been decked out to fetch a pretty price. The walls were peacock blue. There were silver mirrors and candelabras on the walls, furry flokati rugs on the hardwood floors, sleek modern furniture, a fifty-four-inch flat screen ...

Jeans shrieked and threw herself down on the couch: "We reach!" she bawled out, and we all laughed. We put down our heavy knapsacks filled with foodstuffs to last us a good while, and I went to work plugging the door lock with Krazy Glue.

I texted the rest of the team. "You in?" They all replied in the affirmative. We began sending pics to each other of our new digs, comparing furniture, amenities, views. It was a freakin' riot. Jeremy said he had even found a welcoming bottle of Canadian champagne in the fridge.

Suddenly, I remembered the banner. While Pooky and Jeans were busy taking selfies, I went out onto the balcony, in the frigid December air, and secured our banner with ropes to the railings. Over she went. A big, stinking flame. *Take that, motherfuckers.*

Pretty soon I began to see the news feeds coming across my social media. "Multiple Alarms Pulled at Downtown Condos." "Police Trying to Make Sense of Massive Action." "Multiple Banners Unfurled from Downtown Condo Balconies." We tuned into CP24 on the television. To see it played out like that live on TV was pretty impressive. I saw so many of our massive — Joe Snakes and Terry from New Brunswick, Lila and her dog, and of course Rex — playing out on that fifty-four-inch screen. Members from HQ were broadcasting (from an undisclosed location) live on Facebook, talking about our demands.

Pooky and Jeans were whooping and hollering about the place, flicking the lights off and on. All of a sudden we saw the lights in other condos flipping off and on too! Some of them had Movement banners, but some didn't. What the fuck was going on?

For the next two days, the entire city was fixated on us. Round-the-clock coverage, videos going viral, international headlines, Torontonians taking sides. Some newscasters estimated our numbers to be in the hundreds, some in the thousands. Residents of the occupied buildings were interviewed almost hourly, it seemed. By day three most of us were starting to run out of food. We now had to rely on those on the ground — members of the Movement who had been unable or unwilling to take part in the occupation, and sympathetic Torontonians who supported our cause. Each unit's occupiers had walked with a substantial amount of rope; we now lowered this from our balconies to people who waited below with baskets full of food and other necessities. They attached the rope to the basket and we hauled those babies up!

It took a while for the media to figure out what we were up to, but once they did, ordinary people started to get involved. In one Liberty Village condo, some douchebag filmed himself with a giant pair of shears cutting a supply rope, claiming he was doing it "in the name of all things decent." Meanwhile, on the Waterfront, residents of one building started *collecting* baskets full of goodies for us, and they waited outside in the cold hoping someone would see them and throw down a rope. There were definitely some "good Samaritans" here who were looking for Instagram fame or a TikTok moment. The media started to lap it up. In front of several prominent condos, news crews set up shop, hoping to catch some of the action.

On day five, drones began hovering outside occupied condos. We didn't know who was sending these. Toronto Police? Media? RCMP? Certain members of the Movement were afraid for their safety. Some people who had claimed to be "do or die" at the beginning were now caving. It got so bad that a couple of Movement members rappelled down a building in CityPlace and disappeared into the night.

On day seven, rumours began flying that a cell in Fort York had taken a property manager hostage. I also heard that an intra-ethnic beef had broken out amongst South Asians in the Shangri-La condo building in CityPlace. There were condo owners and residents who were recent immigrants, refugee claimants, and desis from India, Pakistan, Sri Lanka, and Bangladesh, and there were members of the Movement who were the same. The main difference between them was that one side had bank and safe, secure, upscale housing, and the other side had nothing to lose. Instead of helping their less fortunate compatriots, the Brown condo contingent began attacking and sabotaging the occupiers. These wealthy model immigrants, doctors and lawyers and bankers, banded together and made it their mission to stop all supplies from reaching the occupiers in their building. They stood in front of the TV cameras talking about what a disgrace and shame these people were, how they brought a bad name to the South Asian community in Canada, and how these occupiers were really just lazy criminal types who thought resorting to violence was the only solution. The Brown occupiers responded by finding out where in the Shangri-La these kiss-asses lived and started strategically dumping feces on their balconies (using the same ropes). It was getting ugly really quickly.

So today it's day ten, and this morning on the news it said that police started using battering rams in one Fort York building.

Some sympathetic peeps — respite workers, mental health advo-
cates, even some professors from Toronto Metropolitan University
and U of T — have formed a human chain around the building.
They are trying to get other sympathizers to do the same so that
at least some of the buildings will become "safe buildings." Not
sure if our building is next on the police list. To be honest, I'm
surprised we lasted this long. The condo residents and the city are
still divided over what should happen. A lot of the condo residents,
especially those who are owners, are *really* upset that this has been
going on so long, like they can't understand why the police won't
just shoot the locks off and shoot us too. I feel like they prefer to
have their property full of bullet holes and blood than to let us stay
here. The novelty seems to have worn off for Pooky and Jeans too.
They've started quarrelling, and last night Pooky threatened to
jump off the balcony, talkin bout how she didn't want to have to go
back to a shelter, or to jail (where she's already been, so she should
know). Looks like the honeymoon's over.

I'd been hoping I could at least spend Christmas here. Just to
be able to gaze out floor-to-ceiling windows Christmas Eve and see
all those twinkling lights on all those balconies, the fully decorated designer Christmas trees strategically placed by the sliding glass
doors for maximum visual effect. I just wanted a moment like that,
to pose up by my window and feel like I was a part of something
bigger than me, something shared, however fake. We coulda had a
family Christmas, me, Pooky, and Jeans, and maybe we, too, could
have posted a *Merry Christmas!* on Instagram, with a nineteenth-
floor, shining, sparkly, glass-box-in-the-sky view, just like all these
other motherfuckers.

Amberine

She had heard the stories of Chacachacare Island from her mother. How an aunt had been disappeared in the middle of the night. The child was found to have leprosy, and the family did their best to hide her at home for as long as possible, taking the risk of the bacteria invading their own organisms. Eventually, the authorities found out, and so contagion, in the body of an eight-year-old child, was discreetly shipped off to the leprosarium on the rocky island of Chacachacare in the Bocas del Dragón. Amberine's mother said that her own mother had cried every day after that, gouged by the guilt of abandoning her child to disfigurement and death. Forbidden from visiting the island, the family never saw Amberine's aunt again.

This particular family history haunted Amberine, but she had heard so many other stories about Chacachacare and the leprosarium that were not much different. Parents carrying small children by boat from the mainland to the island, then leaving them there, on the dock, while they reboarded the vessel and headed back to the mainland, abandoning them, the children screaming and hysterical while the nuns, who had been tasked with caring for the lepers, held them back from hurling themselves into the sea in a desperate attempt to swim after the boat. The most devastating story Amberine had heard was regarding the inception of the island leprosarium. Prior to that, there had been one built on the mainland, but the authorities wanted to isolate the lepers as far away as possible from the general population, because in 1920s Trinidad leprosy was spreading rapidly. The original leprosarium had been situated in a small coastal village, and when the lepers learned of the plan to shunt them away, ostracized on an island prison, incapable of remaining in contact with their families, many panicked. Three hundred lepers, it is said, fled the institution in an attempt to evade the evacuation, but they were captured and sent back to the leprosarium. Realizing the possibility of another mass exodus, the authorities kept the transfer date a secret. One December day in 1921, police surrounded the leprosarium and, amid screams and panic, forced the lepers onto boats and disappeared them to Chacachacare Island. The mainland leprosarium was burnt to the ground, a final banishment of any trace or memory of the roughly five hundred people who had carved out a home there.

Amberine hoped it wouldn't come to that now that The Scourge had created similar panic and terror the globe over. That those deemed contagion, especially those who were unwafered, would find themselves disappeared in the middle of the night, shunted away like pestilence and taken far from their loved ones. From her perspective, The Scourge was an inevitability, nature's way of restoring balance, so what was all the fuss about? Still, so many people had been coming to her since the beginning of the pandemonium, in deep fear spun into hysteria fuelled by press conferences and newspaper statistics and social media campaigns. People came, desperate for prevention and cure, seeking root tonics, tisanes, ointments and unguents, supplements, inhalants, prescriptions for sea baths. Then the government — ostensibly to limit The Scourge — closed the beaches. Forbade access to the rivers. *The mothers will be very upset,* she thought. At other times she would ponder, *Are we being punished? Are Ochun and Yemaya just so fed up with humanity that they are letting us sow the seeds of our own destruction?* She then noticed the repeated reports of drownings in the news: a young woman washed away at the foot of a virulent waterfall during a hike; two men whose boat capsized at sea, their bodies surfacing days later, bloated and bleached white; a child whose parent forgot about them in a full-on rainy season downpour, the child flushed down a box drain like detritus.

For months she had been dreaming The Scourge, long before it became internationally known, long before people's entire existences were taken up with the running commentary displayed on the neon billboards that wrapped around multiple buildings and lit up the highways and main roads, proclaiming death rates, updated hourly. There were also the Integrated Alerts issued every hour from which one could not escape (they jolted mobile phones awake and invaded laptop screens; in some neighbourhoods they were announced from loudspeakers mounted high atop light poles, broadcast at set times like the Adhan, the Muslim call to prayer), alerts on the status of The Scourge, followed by the beautiful music and songs in praise of wafers. Everywhere one looked now — sides of vehicles and buildings, television, internet, newspapers — populations were being saturated with images of sightless eyes and frozen limbs, the most common effects of The Scourge. In her dreams, prior to the pandemonium, Amberine had seen corpses lining the streets, falling down hills, radiating iridescent like cobalt, polluting and festerous. But she never felt fear. She recognized The Scourge as part of the cycle of time; she had seen this day coming, like living next to a volcano for one's entire life and not being in the least surprised when that volcano rumbled, then shook, and finally spewed its lava, destructive yet cleansing.

The day when the pleasant Ministry of Health officials came to her gate and offered her a wafer, she politely declined. They smiled at her benignly as if she were a trained chimp and offered her several glossy pamphlets with pictures of wafers shining like the sun, wafers dressed up in costumes, wafers with anthropomorphic features. She took their pamphlets, bid them good day, went back inside her house, and lit the pamphlets on fire in a small metal trashcan.

That was the first visit.

About a week later, two different Ministry of Health officials appeared at her gate. These ones were not pleasant. Even their uniforms were different, resembling much more the black and dark blue of police uniforms, with shiny brass buttons and epaulettes. Amberine bid them good day and the female official immediately launched into her speech: "We understand up to now you haven't consumed a wafer. You know about The Scourge, right? A woman your age can't be messing around in the pandemonium we in. We brought you a wafer, just to make it easy on you. Here." And she ruffled in the black doctor's bag she had brought with her and produced a packaged wafer, hermetically sealed and strangely resembling a condom in its wrapper.

Amberine had to stifle a laugh at the packaging, and the big, beefy male companion of the female official frowned, grunted, coughed, and scraped his feet on the pavement. *Like a blasted Percheron horse*, Amberine mused.

She wondered if she should just take the wrapped wafer to get rid of them. Set it, too, on fire like the pamphlets. But then she realized they would never be satisfied with that and would insist she consume it in front of them.

"No, thanks."

The female official shifted her doctor's bag from one arm to the other and switched the weight on her legs, extending the left now instead of the right. Amberine noticed that the woman's shoes had no support, some beige ballet slippers from which the woman's feet were bulging, and she had bunions to boot. *She must be in a lot of pain,* Amberine thought, *with her weight and having to walk around all day in those shoes, distributing these damn wafers.*

Before the female official could start up again, Amberine interjected. "Ma'am, would you like a seat?"

The male official grunted again and pulled himself upright, as if to say, "We are fine, and strong, and we are doing our work."

But the female official was caving. Amberine could see the sweat on her brow, her upper lip. She had on a big curly weave. *Under all that hair yuh brains mus be hot.*

Amberine moved swiftly and retrieved a wooden fold-up chair from her gallery. She carried it quickly to the gate, unfolded it, and rested it on the strip of grass bordering her wall. "Here." She gestured.

The female official sat down, just in time it seemed, as she wavered when she sat, momentarily losing her balance. The male official moved quickly to steady her, and after a moment the female official was able to rummage through the plastic bag she had been carrying, producing a bottle of water. She drank a few sips and then, pulling a washcloth from the doctor's bag, fanned herself with it. "It making rell hot," she said.

"Ent."

"I didn't even realize I was feeling so faint!"

Amberine said nothing. It was yet another moment in her life when she had done something or said something without knowing how she knew how to do or say that exact thing.

The male official, who had been mute during this exchange, suddenly excused himself to go smoke a cigarette under the shade of a nearby mango tree.

The female official took this opportunity to reveal to Amberine that she had recently miscarried a baby.

"How long ago?"

"Three weeks."

"An you out here pounding this pavement in this hot sun?"

Even as she said it, Amberine regretted saying it. What options did this woman have? She couldn't have taken a sick leave longer than a few days. Nobody cared that her body was a mess of hormones, having to revert back to its pre-pregnancy state. Never mind the grief the woman must be enduring.

"You ever take anything since then to … you know … clean out?"

"Clean out?"

"Yes, clean out your womb. Make sure everything that needs to shed is shed."

The female official looked at the ground, then at her doctor's bag, and finally at Amberine. "No."

Amberine got up. She said, "Wait here."

She went into her house and rummaged around in her cupboards, in refrigerator doors, placing dried leaves, flowers, roots, and bark in an old jam jar. She came back outside and handed the female official the jar. "Here."

"What's this?"

"Womb cleanser tea. It will help clean out your womb but also help balance out your hormones."

The female official held the bottle, contemplating it. Amberine wondered if she was going to hand it back to her, or worse, dash it to the ground. But all she quietly said was, "Thank you," and when her eyes met Amberine's again, there were tears there. She put the bottle in her doctor's bag.

The male official was walking back toward them, having completed his smoke. The female official got up, thanked Amberine again, and bid her a good day. The two officials then left, walking slowly and steadily down the path leading to the main road.

After that, no officials came to bother Amberine about wafers again.

It was a month later that the WhatsApp message came from Myron: *Mudda ah goin an protest. Pray fuh me.*

Protest where? How? Amberine thought. *What trouble had dis chile gotten himself into in de White people country?*

She knew Myron had been going through a bad time. A really bad time. First the college where he worked as a part-time music instructor had insisted that everyone provide proof of wafer consumption (WC) or there would be consequences. Myron told her he didn't want to take any wafer, he didn't know what was in the wafer, what sort of chemicals they had dropped on the wafer and what it might do to him. He had heard that some people who took the wafer had seizures and died instantly. Other people, he had heard, got very foggy brained and lethargic and simply could not get out of bed. Other people, it seemed, had quite sudden personality changes.

"Is like they want you to take a tab of LSD, Mudda," he had told her. "I don't want to trip out. I don't know what kind of experiments they are trying out on us. Look at Tuskegee, the forced sterilizations of Black and Brown women, medical experimentation on little Indigenous kids in residential schools, even the original goddamn smallpox blankets!"

Amberine had listened and advised him to pray on it and be directed accordingly.

Myron's situation only got more intense. His workplace terminated his contract (on the basis of "non-compliance") and his union would not back him up. Thankfully, he had always had his music and his art as a fallback position — but now he found that the venues where he had played music and sold his art no longer wanted him on the premises (they had become Safer Wafer Zones). The quarrels with his wife of ten years worsened. She was wafered, had lined up diligently as soon as the wafers were handed out (there were two kinds of wafer — Sanctify and Thanos — and she had chosen the former). Myron and Samantha argued endlessly about whether or not their kids would take wafers too, once a child version was made available. It got so bad that as funds in the household dwindled, and Samantha was shouldered with being the sole breadwinner, she suggested Myron move out until he "got himself together."

Ah dohn know what is happening Mudda, he had texted her. *If it wasn't for Ana and BeeBee I mighta done mehself in by now. Ah dohn know that this is a world ah want to live in again.*

Amberine had prescribed several baths with bitter herbs, salt, lime, and tobacco. Even though it would be hard for Myron to find some of the herbs in Toronto in March, she knew he would leave no stone unturned in trying to source them. He was deeply committed to his spiritual practice. For this she loved him as if he were her own son.

Now Myron was homeless. He managed to link with his like-minded friend Atlas and Atlas's girlfriend, Emilie — both of whom were also unwafered — and he lived in their basement for a few weeks, trying to keep his spirits up, trying to live in a society that had suddenly turned on him in a very hateful and unexpected way. He tried to stay away from social media, avoid the news, avoid public spaces where he could be bombarded with constant and never-ending messages about The Scourge, so he spent most of his time focusing on his music and his art and tried not to walk into the frigid waters of the Humber River.

When he went to pick up his daughters one weekend, Samantha informed him that she had already placed an order with the pharmacy for two wafers for Ana and BeeBee, as the Ministry of Health had declared wafers safe and consumable for all children ages five to eighteen. Myron had a sudden urge to take his daughters that day and run, run into the bush, run across the border, jump in a car and drive drive drive to some remote town where they could hide out until the pandemonium was over, until it was safe to raise children again and make art and teach critical thought and paint in protest against injustice and just live a life of creative resistance.

Instead, he took Ana and BeeBee back to his basement apartment and left them with ingredients for a homemade vegan pizza (their dinner that night). He knocked on the adjoining door to the upstairs of the house, where Atlas and Emilie lived. He had decided it was time to take some kind of action rather than lie on his couch day after day, and so he invited Atlas and Emilie to join him in artistic protest.

The couple were down once they heard Myron's plan to produce T-shirts with a variety of slogans. So far he had come up with four ideas:

> *I VOMITED THE WAFER*
> *Am I Sanctified or Human?*
> *Sanctified or Unsanctified?*

The last idea had three check boxes next to three words:

❑ *Sanctified*
❑ *Thanosed*
❑ *Human*

The idea was to recruit people to wear the T-shirts and then engage in mass sit-ins in restaurants, classrooms, malls, banks — places that were Safer Wafer Zones. Protestors would need to feign wafered status to gain entry, but once inside they would drop the jacket or coat they had worn to hide the protest T-shirt and loudly announce, "*I am unwafered!*" Protestors could also stand up and shout in more generally public spaces like airports and the halls of government.

Myron and his fellow protestors decided their first target would be the Dundas Square Shopping Centre in the heart of the city. People, despite the pandemonium, were frantically pelting out thousands of dollars for clothes, electronics, alcohol, and recreational drugs (which were readily available just outside the mall), in a blind and desperate attempt to distract themselves from the reality of the pandemonium and the constant bombardment of fear-inducing media updates. It was on the verge of panic buying because one never knew if or when the government would lock down the stores again, so people consumed in a frenzy, quickly maxing out credit cards, compounding their stress and hopelessness.

There were twenty protestors that Tuesday morning, indistinguishable from all the other mall patrons in their giant parkas and duffle coats. They moved swiftly to the centre of the food court where, grabbing an opportunity, two of the protestors suddenly jumped up on a table.

Oh no, Myron thought instantly. *This was not part of the plan!*

Two others (young Gen Zers who were enthralled with participating in Real Live Protest for the first time) jumped on the plastic chairs welded to the tables, and flanked the table toppers. With great flair, the four threw off their outer garments and shouted out the slogans on their shirts:

"I ... am ... unwaaaaaafeeeeeered!"

"Sanctified or huuuuuumaaaaan?!"

People immediately whipped out their cellphones and began recording. Myron, Atlas, and Emilie, in another part of the food court, also threw off their coats and began chanting the slogans on their T-shirts. Within minutes, a few security guards had arrived and moved swiftly to the protestors — big, White, beefy security guardsmen who clearly saw this as an opportunity to flex their muscles. While Myron had been very careful to coach everyone in nonresistance, one of the Gen Zers began to tussle with the security guard; this led to the security guard — equal in height and weight to the protestor — to actually sit on the outraged Gen Zer. The impromptu paparazzi reacted strongly to this, and more and more spectators pressed forward, some now jumping up on the food court chairs and tables, others raising their cellphones above the heads of those standing in front of them, while even more security began to appear, descending on the scene to keep the ever-increasing crowds back from the protestors. As the energy rose, it seemed many in the crowd were supportive of Myron and his cohorts. Myron could hear someone shouting, "Let them go!" and another person was arguing with a security guard that these people had a right to peaceful protest. Someone else started a chant — "Racist rent-a-cops! Racist rent-a-cops!" — which quickly picked up momentum. And then the police arrived.

The way Myron recounted the events to Amberine, the police were very quick to handcuff him, Atlas, Emilie, and the others and whisk them swiftly out of the basement doors of the mall, those that led to the parking garage. There they were ushered into a police van and sent off to headquarters, which was only a few blocks away.

They have us here in a cell Mudda. They letting us keep our cellphones, so I guess they are monitoring everything I typin.

Amberine did not like this at all. Anything could happen to Myron now that he was locked up.

When she went to sleep that night, she had a dream. She dreamt that a giant butterfly, pink and coral and yellow in its hues, bore her up and up and up, and she felt so free, so beautiful and free, and totally protected between the butterfly's giant wings. The next part of the dream, she was in Toronto, and it was a brilliant winter morning after a fresh snowfall, the sun reflecting blindingly off the intense whiteness, a snap to the air, that damp smell of wet and ice, the feeling that just now the brand-new snowfall would be dropping in clumps off the trees, melting in the radiant sun. Her mother appeared to her just then in a knee-length fur coat, and she seemed perturbed. Amberine asked her mother where she was going, and her mother replied, "SickKids Hospital." Amberine knew the hospital well: as a mother raising two children in downtown Toronto, she had attended that hospital more than once, sometimes for minor things, sometimes for more than minor things.

Amberine woke up with a longing to see her two children. They were both grown now, busy, adulting, immersed in careers and families and commitments. While she had stayed in touch with both of them, since the pandemonium their relationships had become more strained and distant, especially over the topic of wafers. Amberine was not sure if her children, and their partners, had wafered to keep their jobs or because they really believed wafering was good, necessary, and sacrosanct. The fact that she had remained unwafered bothered both of them to no end. She even wondered if between the two of them they were questioning her mental well-being, whether or not she was displaying signs of early onset Alzheimer's. Who knows? Maybe they were already deciding how they would deal with her should she lose her marbles thousands of miles away from them.

It wasn't just her children, along with Myron, that had her thinking about a return to Toronto, however brief. The fact that her mother had shown up to her in her dream, and had *not* looked pleased, meant that she needed to visit that woman's particular grave. It was the one thing Amberine had regretted — never collecting any soil from her mother's grave when she had left Canada for good, to go live in "the islands" (as Canadians would say). "The islands": a nondescript region of all-inclusive resorts and rum punches and white sand beaches and sexy men and women and cruise-ship ports of call and piña coladas and palm trees. A picture-postcard, subway-ad, TV-commercial fallacy so far removed from Amberine's reality, yet even when she tried to explain this to her Canadian co-workers and neighbours, her explanations always fell flat, and she would have to hear, yet again, how "jealous" people were that she lived there. "I'm so jelly!" became the cry. Amberine let out a big sigh just anticipating what she would be in for when and if she paid Toronto a visit, as it now seemed she might be inclined to do. But how could she really travel? As an unwafered person, travelling seemed out of the question at worst, extremely difficult and harrowing at best. Then she remembered the butterfly of her dream.

•

IN TRUTH, THE STATE AUTHORITIES HAD BEEN WATCHING Myron for some time, intercepting his social media chats and posts, keeping track of his work dismissal and wafer status. They had even been monitoring his estranged wife and children. The Canadian state had decided at this particular juncture that the most efficacious way of dealing with the Myrons of society was to "radically re-socialize" and "re-educate" them. So when Myron and his cohort were arrested, the police allowed them to keep their cellphones at first. They wanted the protestors to let their guard down. It was strategy: they thought this would build a level of trust with their captives.

When Myron messaged Amberine that the authorities were "interrogating" him and that he was being taken for daily "re-education sessions," something in her suddenly converged, and she snapped into action. She got the stool from the kitchen and reached high atop the built-in teak wardrobe in the bedroom to get her suitcase. She went online and purchased a return ticket to Toronto — one week only; any longer and it could become dangerous for her. When she reached the section of the online form where it asked if she was wafered or not, she instinctively clicked YES. She didn't know why she did that, but spirit had instructed her to do so, and so she obeyed.

Amberine messaged her two children and let them know when she would be arriving and when she would be departing. She did not message Myron any of this information. She checked the expiry date on her Canadian passport and washed, dried, and packed all her winter clothes, which had been put away for years. As the date of her departure approached, she began to take a variety of spiritual baths. She manufactured amulets and resguardos and gris-gris. She prayed.

Finally, the day of departure came. Amberine took a car to the airport, wheeled her luggage up to the check-in counter, and met the attendant.

"Good afternoon. Where are you flying to today?"

"Toronto."

"May I see your passport, please?"

Amberine handed over her Canadian passport. The attendant clicked away on the keyboard.

"How many pieces of luggage are you checking in today?"

"One."

The attendant peered over the counter. "Can you put the suitcase up on the scale for me, please?"

Amberine lifted the tiger-striped suitcase onto the scale. She knew the suitcase was bold and stood out and she didn't care. *Maferefun Changó.*

The attendant continued clicking away on the keyboard. Within seconds she was affixing the travel sticker to Amberine's suitcase. She then handed Amberine's passport back to her.

"Please be at gate twenty-three by one thirty p.m. Boarding starts at two p.m."

"All right, thank you."

"Enjoy your flight."

Had the attendant forgotten? Wasn't she supposed to ask Amberine for proof of wafering? Amberine was a bit confused, but knew better than to question it further. She proceeded to the first security checkpoint. As she pushed her way through the revolving glass doors, she could see that the security guard was bepping at his post, nodding off, his cap precariously perched on his head at an almost impossible angle. *What to do?* Amberine hesitated for mere seconds, then pushed her way boldly through the next set of revolving doors before the security guard awoke. She was now in the duty-free mall preceding the next security checkpoint.

When she arrived at the second checkpoint, there was not much of a lineup, and neither were there many security personnel working. Amberine noticed two male and one female security personnel working the X-ray machine and conveyor belts. She also noticed that they were in hot discussion; apparently, some co-worker had been caught tiefing on the job and was now embroiled in disciplinary action with the airport authority. As Amberine placed her knapsack onto the conveyor belt and then took off her white shoes and placed them on the belt as well, the three security personnel were so distracted by their conversation that no one bothered to even check her passport, or remember to watch the screen as her luggage passed through the X-ray machine.

"Well, you know what de ole people say: tief tief from tief make god laugh!"

"Ah tell yuh!"

"But dem is de biggest tieffff bwoy! Yuh ever see Allan car? Ah mean cars? One day he drivin a Lexus, next day is a Porsche, next day is a Hummer ..."

"An nevah mine de two beach house, one een de north and one een de sout — plus de luxury condo een de west!"

Amberine behaved as if she were invisible. She collected her knapsack and shoes on the other side of the X-ray machine, quickly slipped on the white loafers, and proceeded down the corridor to the departure lounge. She could hear the three security personnel buss out in uproarious laughter behind her, one bawling, "An if you seeee de horner woman! Nah bwoy!"

It was now 1:45 p.m. Fifteen minutes until boarding. Amberine went into a souvenir store and bought some bottled water, chewing gum, and chocolate-covered peanuts. At the gate, she found a seat not far from the counter. The airline staff were already busying themselves, setting up, getting ready to welcome the passengers on board. Unlike the security personnel she had just encountered, these employees seemed sharp, businesslike, focused. Amberine began to finger her elekes, the sacred necklaces she wore whenever she travelled. She began praying to specific spirits.

There was a couple seated a few rows ahead of her. The woman was ruffling through her carry-on luggage, anxiously looking for something. The man seemed upset, even angered, by this. "For godssakes, people are looking!" Amberine heard him say. She averted her eyes, but she could still hear them.

The woman said, "Well, all I can say is, thank god I am getting back to civilization where people accept the wafer and are sane! I am finally getting away from these unwafered masses!"

The man responded, "Look, no one told you you had to come! It was my mother who got sick —"

"Oh right, and if I hadn't come I would have never heard the end of it! Your family —"

"Don't start about my family."

"Your family and their contagion! No wonder your mother got sick!"

Out of the corner of her eye, Amberine could see the man had gotten up and was walking away in the direction of the washrooms.

Amberine looked back at the airline staff. They were starting to make the pre-boarding announcements. "Please ensure that your passport and wafer documents are open to the photo ID page." She bowed her head, fingered her elekes again, repeating her prayer.

When she raised her head, she saw the airplane pulling up to the passenger boarding bridge, and she noticed a beautiful orange, mauve, and coral–coloured butterfly painted on its side, part of the airline's logo. She smiled.

When it came time to board, the same quarrelling couple began to argue with one of the staff at the gate. It got loud — Amberine thought she even heard a cuss word or two. Some of the airline staff members had to excuse themselves from checking passenger documentation to assist their embattled co-worker. This left one lone attendant to check the documentation of the remaining passengers.

When the attendant came face to face with Amberine, she exclaimed, "Oh, what lovely necklaces!" Amberine thanked her. It was as if the woman was transfixed. She barely flipped Amberine's passport open and closed, then waved her on. "Enjoy the flight!"

Hours later, Amberine arrived at Pearson International Airport. As she disembarked the plane, she noticed two heavily armed security guards checking people's passports as they exited the airbridge. She knew this had to do with undocumented migrants and not wafers, and even though she had her passport in her hand, the two robotic men glanced through her as if she were invisible and never asked to see her documentation.

It was a long walk to the immigration floor. The first thing that struck Amberine was the number of White people in the airport. There were so many. She had not been around this many White people in years, and it startled her. And it wasn't just the White people who, like her, were walking through the lengthy passageway to immigration; it was the gigantic advertisements everywhere, lining the walls, hanging from the ceiling, populated with images of wealthy, thin White people. People who looked wealthy from the clothes they wore, the activities they were engaged in, the things they were buying. She had forgotten how prevalent this was, the constant messaging, the in-your-face erasure.

When she finally reached the banks of automated passport checking machines on the immigration floor, she was guided by an attendant to the appropriate line. There were a lot of people waiting, but finally, she arrived at the head of the line and saw a green light atop one of the scanning machines indicating it was available. She inserted her passport and the machine immediately spit it out. She squinted a bit to read the instructions on the screen, thinking maybe she had inserted the passport incorrectly. She tried again. Same thing. She waved over one of the nearby attendants. It was a Jamaican woman, who, Amberine noted, was clearly frustrated with her job.

"Wha'appen?"

"It's not taking my passport. It keeps spitting it out."

"Hawlright. Old on." The woman took Amberine's passport and tried it herself. The machine spit it out again. The woman let out one loud, long *cheeuupssss*. "Miss, you haffi go in de line to de farrrr lef for personal hinspekshun, hawlright?"

Amberine nodded, thanked her, and moved to the line furthest left. It was a short line, and she quickly came face to face with another beefy, burly, surly, heavily armed border guard. He barked at her. "Passport and proof of wafering!"

She handed him her passport, and began to pray.

The man kept looking at her passport, and then her face, her passport, and then her face. Finally, he said, "Where did you get the *Chong*?"

"Excuse me?" Amberine was baffled. Her last name was Chong. Her grandfather had been of Chinese and Portuguese descent. Nothing uncommon by Caribbean standards. She was a mixup callaloo of many heritages.

"The last name *Chong*. Where did you get it from?"

When Amberine finally understood what the guard was asking, and why (clearly, to him her face and name did not match), she pulled herself up, watched him straight in his eye, and said very firmly, "Meh granfadda."

The guard blinked, looked down again at her passport, and then handed it back to Amberine with what she read to be pure disdain. He brushed her off with *"Next!"*

After that, Amberine sailed through the doors leading to the luggage carousels. Her loud-ass tiger-skin suitcase came smoothly down the ramp and stood straight up so that she could easily manoeuvre it off the carousel. She swiftly wheeled it past the very last checkpoint of her journey. Now it was time to find a taxi.

Amberine had rented an Airbnb in the west end of the city, in a neighbourhood she was most familiar with because she had lived there for decades. She messaged her children to let them know she had arrived, and then ordered some food to be delivered. She was wary of walking the streets, unsure of how draconian the authorities were here about the unwafered, unsure if she would be allowed in a restaurant or grocery or even a convenience store.

The next day, Amberine set out to complete her first task, which was to gather the dirt from her mother's grave. To get there she would need to ride at least two subway trains. Although she had not travelled on the TTC metro in years, little had changed. There was still the dank, damp smell in the tunnels, still emaciated mice scurrying along the tracks, still mad people talking to themselves and then asking for money, still the utter frigidity of humans staring past each other, averting their eyes at all costs to avoid human connection or recognition, burying themselves deep in their devices, vex-looking, sour-looking, or simply incapable of consciousness altogether, passed out, their heads lolling though their stop.

Amberine sat in a back-to-back seat. The two women behind her were deep in conversation.

"Did you see on the news that they caught people selling fake wafer documents?"

"Well, I'm not surprised. These people will stop at nothing. They *are* The Scourge! Janice told me they're going to create a snitch line so you can report unwafered people in your neighbour-hood and the government can then put surveillance on them."

"I don't know why they don't just jail them all. They *are* the cause of all the pandemonium and deserve to be put away. Even better, why don't they just put them all on a plane and ship them to some island!"

"Right?"

Amberine was relieved that the next stop was hers. The cemetery was not a far walk from the subway station. The earth on her mother's grave was rich and wet from the accumulated snowfall of the winter that was now coming to an end. Someone had inserted a bouquet of plastic lilies in the dirt — how long ago she had no idea. Amberine knew there was only a small urn in that dirt, and no coffin; an urn that contained the cremated remains of whatever pieces of her mother's body were left after the numerous autopsies that had been performed by medical students at the local university. Her mother had donated her body to science in a last charitable act, hoping that her sacrifice would alleviate the suffering of those with the same affliction she had succumbed to. Amberine wondered what pieces had been cremated in the end. A clavicle? Fingers, hands? Her head? What, if anything, had been left, untouched by inquisitive, intrusive hands?

Amberine talked with her mother on the regular, sometimes while awake but more often in dreams, even though her mother had been dead for over four decades. Standing at this grave was not a prerequisite to holding these conversations. Amberine explained to her mother what she was doing there, why she had come all this way. She asked for her blessings; she asked for blessings for both her children. She collected some of the dirt in a jar, bade her mother farewell, turned around, and did not look back.

The next day, Amberine had arranged to meet both of her grown children in a parking lot not far from her Airbnb. Because she was unwafered, she could not go to her children's homes; she could not meet them in a restaurant or a mall, a store or a museum. So her kids had decided they would each drive their cars and meet her in a parking lot, where they could see each other but not hug or kiss or touch or breathe the same air. It had come to this. Amberine had nothing to say about these arrangements. Her son was a regulator scientist and her daughter taught deductive reasoning at a local college. She had learned to accept their differences, accept that the universe has its own way of arranging patterns and creating balance. From her vantage point, her children were still young in many ways. The three conversed via a WhatsApp group call in the parking lot, Amberine waving and smiling, past the point of tears now, and she saw that her kids were equally stoic, conformed to fear. She had to push down the corporal memory, the bond of blood, flesh, milk, and body heat. She considered how incredible it was that a stupid wafer could just destroy that bond, could so distort it. She blew kisses as her children departed, saying a silent prayer to the Creator that this would not be the last time she saw them.

With the few days she had left in Toronto, she turned her attention to Myron. It seemed obvious that the authorities had now confiscated his cellphone because she had not received any more texts from him since she had left on her trip. Then, to her surprise, Myron called her two days before her departure. Although she did not recognize the number on her phone, something told her she needed to answer. She was glad that she did.

"Mudda?"

"Myron! Where are you?"

"I'm still in jail, Mudda. A celly here got a mobile so I can't talk long. I just wanted to let you know that I am okay."

It didn't sound like Myron. Why did he sound different?

"Myron. Are you okay?"

"Mudda, it's all right. I think ... I think everything is gonna be all right now."

"What is happening with your case? Are they dropping the charges? Did you get a lawyer?"

There was a long pause on the phone. Amberine wondered if they had been disconnected.

"Hello? Myron?"

"Weeeeeellllllll." Myron stretched out the word, as if he was trying to fill gaps, big gaps, in the conversation. "I'm not really worried about that anymore. I think everything is gonna be fine. Don't worry."

What the hell? Amberine was suddenly incensed. Like a mama bear she sprang into action.

"*Myron*. What happened? Did they make you take anything? What have you been eating? What —"

"Mudda, ah hadda go. Stay well."

He was gone.

Since the pandemonium had begun, Amberine had noticed something about the wafered: they became very complacent, apathetic, to the point that they seemed incapable of action, even in the face of obvious injustices. *Zombified*, she had thought after she began to encounter more and more wafered people in her life and had tried to engage them in conversations about social injustice, or discrimination, or divide-and-rule tactics, or dictatorship. Acquaintances who had once been diehard activists, always speaking out about corruption or social ills, suddenly fell silent. She began to wonder if the wafers truly were zombifying people, if the wafer scientists had inserted traces of the poison tetrodotoxin, distilled from the liver and gonads of the puffer fish, into them. She and Myron had engaged in numerous discussions — sometimes ending in uproarious laughter — about the strange behaviour of previously perfectly sane people who had suddenly becoming zombified, dense, slow, servile, and robotic. They had jokingly referred to these people in a state of non-agency as "the Stepfords," after the movie *The Stepford Wives*. Now the phone call with Myron had Amberine wondering if she had reached Toronto too late to help him.

The day before she left Toronto, Amberine completed the ritual for Myron outside the jail.

She went at twilight, walked as close to the imposing building as she dared, and pulled her phone out of her jacket pocket. Pretending to be on a call, she quickly dropped what she had come to drop, kicked some dead leaves over it, then quickly turned and walked off.

Her flight back to the island departed at seven the following morning. As her plane rose higher and higher over Toronto, she watched the tiny houses carefully, seeking out those that she knew intimately, even those that caused a sharp pain in her heart. The others were simply there, innocuous, grains of sand on a seashore. She thought of her children and their wafered lives, and she wondered if, in time, the effects of wafering could wear off, if cells could regenerate, if wholeness could be restored. The houses got smaller and smaller, the plane picked up speed and altitude, and then everything disappeared in wisps and blankets of clouds.

•

IT WAS MYRON'S WIFE SAMANTHA WHO CALLED HER ABOUT A week later. She called to say that after Myron had been released from jail, he had been acting strangely. Three days after his release, he was found hanging from a tree by the river. He didn't leave a note. As Samantha railed on about how his crazy anti-wafer activism had led to all this, sobbing intermittently in her diatribe, all Amberine could think was *He should have come home. He should have come home instead of protesting in that country.* She knew her own children would never leave that country, would never *come home.* Now her spiritual son was lost to her as well.

After Samantha ended the call, Amberine found a white nine-day candle in her cupboard. She cleansed it with Florida water, placed it on her ancestral altar, and lit it. Later she would look for a picture of Myron to place next to it. From a distance, she could hear dogs beginning to howl, at first faintly, but then it picked up, one by one joining in, a howling that traversed the hills, a chorus of wails, until the dogs in her yard joined in, too.

Well, yuh finally reach. Tell me what they did to you, she asked. *I am here, waiting.*

Obfuscation

Dexter had always figured himself a public intellectual. It just went with the territory. Elite school, parents who were lower-middle class and decent, a childhood of well-broughtupsy, a house full of libraries, a mind full of references and analogies, a well-pressed school uniform, after-school lessons, money in the bank for when he wanted to attend "universities." It led to a kind of obnoxious self-importance; a trying to distance himself and be distanced from de bredrens, de fellas on de block. And now, at thirty-five, he was stuck in a conundrum: What was he, after all? What did he really want all those years ago? He would begin the litany in his head (what he imagined would be written about him at some later date, not posthumously, but upon winning some accolade or award); it would begin: *The new world radical*

intellectual, the one lone man who can lead the masses out of dark-
ness, lead the bredren off the corner …

… But then again (the voice in his head continued) *what does*
he really know or care about them? They are what he avoided as he
alighted from his driver's car to get to the good school; they are the
ones he evaded as he walked home late after extracurricular studies,
striving; the ones whose eyes he passed after returning from abroad,
degree in hand. He has been groomed to be a better subject, a better
leader, a leader amongst men, an example; to walk by example, talk
in tones and ways so that only those select few can interpret the true
meaning of his worldliness, his brilliance. He has no time for the
common man; let him chain you up with obfuscation, with drones,
droning in a pattern of meaninglessness that is applauded and award-
ed and extolled as academic brilliance when in fact it only distances
us from ourselves, he from himself, you and I from each other, and
he suffers this painful loneliness that he talks about publicly as if to
draw to himself the ever-present need for human warmth, to remind
himself that he is more than his test scores, than his exam results, his
scholarship, the letters before and behind his name, the chosen one,
the privileged one …

Dexter cultivated his obfuscation. It was a mask behind a
smokescreen behind an Oriental screen in the depths of the bowels
of a cave of his own making. Even he did not know who he was
really portraying. Once, as he studied his image in a mirror, he
swore that his head was actually pulsing, swelling and then con-
tracting, respiring, like some great hydrocephalus that ebbed and
flowed in a jellyfish rhythm. He imagined his brain had grown
too big for his cranium. He loved this idea, but deeply feared and
hated it. What if his genius, his brilliance, leaked out of his skull
and ended up splattering all over his newest publication, his brilliant book, the one he had signed copies of at various lectures and
launches and gatherings in the academic world he inhabited? What
if it all became *too much*? But then he would comfort himself in

the fact that his genius had been recorded already for posterity, so he need not fear obscurity. He would pour himself a shot of twenty-five-year-old single malt whisky (in a crystal goblet, not a glass) and remind himself that *he had arrived*.

Because he appeared so self-assured, Dexter at times acted recklessly. There was the incident behind the door, for instance. He just became so overwhelmed with his own brilliance, and that particular day he saw it reflected back to him through the eyes of his twenty-five-year-old graduate student, Alicia, and so he had impulsively embraced her in a congratulatory manner behind his office door after she successfully defended her thesis. But the embrace went on a little too long for Alicia; she had felt discomfort on seeing him close the door to his office before embracing her, and they were quite alone in there, only the two of them and all his books, his gift to *his people*, his degrees framed on the wall, his awards lining the cabinet, and his own tomes in pride of place between two black Power-to-the-People raised-fist bookends on his ample desk. Alicia had stiffly kept her arms at her side the whole time, and eventually managed to extricate herself from his awkward attempt at … what? Praise? A newly revealed interest in her? Soon thereafter she excused herself, and she made sure she was *never* alone with him again.

But Dexter (Dr. Devonshire to his students) felt he had exhibited great sincerity and sympathy in his affectionate overture. He was sure she had been appreciative of his expression of admiration for all the hard work she had done. He left campus that day feeling exhilarated, confident in the fact that, as a female student of his, she would never need to learn the art of obfuscation. This was beneath women, he thought. Women were guileless, easily read like water meters.

Dexter imagined himself a catch in the vastly unequal world of educated, degreed, and well-earning Caribbean men versus desperate, equally educated, marriageable, and biological clock-ticking

Caribbean women. However, it seemed none of the women he encountered were particularly good enough for him. He needed a woman who would praise him as he praised himself; one smart enough to take to the awards dinners and the convocations and the conferences (sometimes, not all the time, because often these conferences were also for *the boys*, and a certain infantility would take over the middle-aged, increasingly flaccid males as they thirstily pursued adoring and sycophant grad students, their male privilege hanging out of their pants much like their limp pricks); a woman who pressed her hair but never wore press-on nails; one who wore pearls but didn't know what a "pearl necklace" was. These women, the ones he could take home to meet his momma and his aunty, the good girls, clean, educated, and happy to bask in his limelight, seemed to elude him. He dated, yes, but too often the women ended up being as ambitious as he was; they were educated *and* independent; they wanted too much or required too little; they believed they could have marriage, a family, *and* a career. Sometimes in his frustration he would turn to drink and then post pictures on Instagram and Facebook of his publications alongside the twenty-five-year-old single malt Scotch in the glass, captioned with his intellectual musings. One day someone errantly posted on IG that maybe he was a battyman after all, and he convinced himself that he better choose a mate soon and settle down or his reputation might become besmirched.

It was sometime after his fourth book had been published (and roundly applauded by his colleagues both on the island where he lived and in the Caribbean diasporic circles of New York, Toronto, Miami, and London) that he noticed a shift occurring in the conferences he attended. There seemed to be fewer and fewer female graduate students who sat, doe-eyed and enraptured, when he gave his keynote lectures and held his round tables. After the day's work was done and he went down to the hotel bar to unwind, he was hard-pressed to find a table of attractive young women who would eagerly beckon for him to come and sit with them. Instead, what he found were tables of exuberant young men holding court, with shaved-on-the-side hairstyles or locks piled on top of their heads or trimmed at a decent and classy length, wearing flashy bow ties or even cravats, their faces occupied by multiple piercings, some sporting plugs in their ears as well. Fanning and fawning over each other, they slapped high-fives in a way he had never quite seen before. As he passed these tables, all the chitter-chatter would stop, and he could feel the multiple pairs of eyes glued to him, sizing him up. It made him feel uncomfortable. He expressed his discomfort to his colleague and former schoolmate Benton one day, sitting by the pool at the annual Society for West Indian Thought conference, which that year was taking place in Curaçao.

"Bentie boy, I don't know how this happen! Like a whole set of them have just descended on the conferences now."

"Well, yes, Dex, a long time now this is the new thing!"

"I mean, when I went to conferences in Brooklyn and Toronto that wasn't unheard of. But now they appear to be taking over the damn proceedings!"

He realized an angry tone that he hadn't intended had come out with this last comment. It hung in the air like a fart.

Benton contemplated his glass of Scotch, then sipped it slowly.

Dexter continued, "The other day I was asked to peer review for an edited volume on twentieth-century decolonizing movements in the English-speaking Caribbean. I couldn't believe how many" — he paused, searching for the right word — "*queer*-themed submissions there were!" He took a stiff sip of the Glenlivet on the rocks he had ordered. The drink was loosening his tongue, and it felt good. "'Homoerotic Nuances Evident in the Pan-Africanist Movement of the 1950s,' 'Battyman Bonding Among the Garveyites of Harlem,' 'Black Power Buller Brothers: An Investigation of the Gay Undercurrents of Trinidad's 1970s Uprising'!" Dexter shook his head, and shifted his eyes sideways at Benton. "I mean, what de ass!"

Benton burst out laughing. "No pun intended!"

Dexter barely heard his friend's jibe. He was on a roll now. "And let's not even get into the *women*! Always with some nasty, funky dreadlocked hairdo. What happened to *nice, pressed hair*?" For a moment he fondly remembered how beautiful his mother had looked upon returning from the hairdresser's, back when he was a child, her hair neatly and soberly haloing her head like shiny icing on a cake. His father had always complimented his mother after she'd visited the beauty salon. He continued his rant. "Always smelling of patchouli oil, rings *everywhere* — fingers, toes, nose ..." He shook his head emphatically. "Nooooo, Bentie, no. What is happening to our people?"

As if on cue, a youngish woman entered the bar. She had a statuesque presence, a long neck, flowing hair that reached down her back. She was dressed in a simple yellow dress, but it was made out of some material that clung to her shape in a way that was very flattering without being provocative. Bell sleeves added a delicacy and allure that made Dexter suddenly speechless. On her chest was heavy-looking brass jewellery, African-style, and she had a headband that glittered in golden highlights. Dexter thought to himself that she resembled Carmen de Lavallade. A classic beauty.

She was coming right toward them. "Professor Anthropode!" She reached out her long, slim arms to Benton, who beamed with a genuine warmth to see her.

"Jacqueline! How are you, my dear?"

"I am very well! Very well!" Her accent was a mixture of colonial Caribbean, elite schooling, and Americanized twang.

"Fancy meeting you here!"

"Yes, isn't it?"

"How are you enjoying the conference, my dear?"

"Well, I will enjoy it more after Thursday. That's the day I have to present!"

"Oh, which panel is that?"

"The one on Feminist Leanings in Caribbean Diasporic Revolutionary Social Movements."

"Oh. Well, I will try to be there."

"Okay, I will look out for you!" She glanced at Dexter. "Hello. Sorry to interrupt. My name is Jacqueline Bernard." She stuck out her hand.

"Dr. Dexter Devonshire. Pleased to meet you."

"Oh! Professor Devonshire? *The* Professor Devonshire?" Her eyes widened in a way Dexter found alluring.

Benton began chuckling. "What were you saying about the women at these conferences?"

Dexter shot his friend a glance. "Well, I take it all back now! I'm not sure if I am *the* Professor Devonshire … Depends. Is that a good or a bad thing?" He offered her a half smile.

"Oh, a good thing! We studied *All Is Not Lost: Twenty-First Century Musings on the Future of Caribbeing-ness* in my Caribbean thought doctoral class. I actually quoted you several times in my dissertation!"

Dexter felt a familiar stirring in his groin. He was flattered that this young woman had reeled off the lengthy title of one of his most esteemed books. He decided to tell her so, when —

"*Jackeeeeeeeeee!! Ja-kay-kay-kay-kay!*"

"*Sa*-valon!"

One of the exuberant young men was dashing toward Jacqueline, arms outstretched, weaving back and forth in what Dexter could only assume was some kind of Watusi mating ritual. He felt instantly jealous. To his horror, Jacqueline began to reciprocate, weaving her body and head from side to side, stalking up on this dude Savalon. People turned to watch the pair. Savalon had on a jumbo black bow tie, some kind of blue velvet 1970s tuxedo jacket, and oversized Gucci glasses. The pair's antics were quite the sight. They finally embraced, laughing heartily. Dexter was too far away to hear what they were saying, but he did see Jacqueline gesture toward him. Savalon nodded and smoothed his hair, and the two walked over to Dexter and Benton.

"Dr. Devonshire, I'd like you to meet my good friend Savalon X-chequer."

Dexter simply nodded at Savalon, who had already stuck out his hand.

"Savalon is going to be *the* greatest new thing in Caribbean and Black cultural queer studies!" Jacqueline was gushing.

Savalon smirked, adjusted his bow tie. "Well, if you say so, sweetie!" Then he turned to Dexter. "Such a pleasure meeting you. Your work is brilliant. Simply brilliant." He paused. "But I'm just wondering … why there is no queer analysis in it? Like, I know, as a gay man reading it, I'm always, like, *where am I?* You know?"

Dexter could not believe the audacity of this young man. Fresh out of grad school and ready to take on the major leagues. The nerve.

"Well, I guess that's the book *you're* going to write," he said snidely.

Savalon laughed nervously, only now realizing he'd hit a nerve. He suddenly threw his arm around Jacqueline's waist. "*We're* going to write!" he proclaimed triumphantly.

Jacqueline looked confused. "We are?" she said.

"Yes! It will be brilliant! I'm going to write the queer part and *you're* going to bring all your feminist misogynoir sass!" He chuckled deeply to himself. "Oh, *honey!*" he exclaimed, clutching the non-existent pearls. "It's gonna be a *bestseller!*"

Jacqueline smiled graciously now. She realized that all this was part of a performance for Dr. Devonshire. "Well, I'm *sure* it won't be as epic as Dr. Devonshire's work!" she said diplomatically.

Dexter raised his glass to her. She lowered her eyes a bit at him. Just a bit. He liked that. He could feel some chemistry between them. He needed to get rid of her "boyfriend."

"Shall we drink to it? What's everybody drinking? Bartender!"

Dexter gestured toward the bartender, who was preoccupied at the other end of the bar.

Benton, realizing his cue, moved to make room for Jacqueline to sit between himself and Dexter. He turned to Savalon, introducing himself, and the two engaged in some conversation. Eventually, Savalon excused himself to go back to his group, promising to attend Jacqueline's panel on Thursday.

Halfway through the first drink, Dexter invited Jacqueline to call him by his first name instead of Dr. Devonshire ("Let's do away with formalities, shall we?"). By the third drink, Benton, feeling like a third wheel, excused himself to go back to his room. By the end of the fourth drink and while waiting for the fifth, Jacqueline noticed that the bar was emptying out, that the waiters were starting to upend chairs on tables. She suddenly realized that drinking with an esteemed professor this late, just the two of them, might result in the inevitable conference gossip, and she told him that this would be her last drink and that she really needed to get some sleep to be fresh for the panels the next day. He impulsively took her hand and she didn't resist. Truth was, she didn't want to leave. He was fascinating, and he exuded a kind of confidence that prophesized a strong sex drive. To her, he was a real man. She hadn't met one of these in a while.

Dexter was surprised at this young woman's intellect. It was quite impressive, given that she was also nice to look at. But besides her intellect, he kept studying her composure. Her demureness. Her decorum. Even though they were drinking, she always maintained her sobriety, it seemed. She got a bit flushed in the face the more she drank, and once she giggled a bit loudly when he told an off-colour joke. But she was very ... *manicured.* She was a real lady. He hadn't met one of those in a while.

When he took her hand, it surprised even him. But he felt if he did not make his move now, she might get away.

"What are you doing after the conference?" he asked.

"You mean, after the panel tomorrow?"

"No, I mean when the conference ends on Friday. Are you leaving right away, or are you staying?"

Many conference participants liked to stay a few days after the proceedings were over, to have a mini-vacation or do some sightseeing. He was hoping she would be amongst them.

"I'm staying until Sunday night. I wanted to try to do some research. Not sure when I will ever return to Curaçao."

Dexter had a flight booked for Saturday morning. He suddenly wanted to change it. He wasn't due back to his office on the university campus in Barbados until Monday morning.

He played with her fingers a bit. She hadn't drawn her hand away. Not at all.

"Well, maybe we can do something together after the conference?"

If Jacqueline's panties had not been wet before, they certainly were now. She imagined the two of them in some Hilton hotel room, somewhere where no conference people could find them, he giving her solid backshot while he pulled on her long hair, she cocking up her bamsee in the bed, wet sheets all over the floor, shades drawn. She blushed.

"That sounds good."

•

IT HAD BEEN TWO YEARS SINCE THE WEDDING IN ST. JAMES Parish Church. The lace in Jacqueline's Edwardian-style wedding dress had matched the limestone of the interior. It wasn't an extravagant wedding by any means, but the who's who of the Bajan academic elite were there, as were a few of Dexter's former schoolmates, including Bentie Anthropode, who joked at the reception that had it not been for him, this union would have never come to fruition. Jacqueline had also invited a number of her former school friends from Howard to fly in, including Savalon. He brought his plus-one (a slight, Indo-Caribbean fellow who kept his shades on through the entire service and only took them off to wine up the dance floor at the reception), and he also brought all the gossip from the circle of people he and Jacqueline had in common; this had her in stitches through most of the night.

For the entire three-and-a-half years that Dexter had been with Jacqueline, he'd had no choice but to accept her close friendship with Savalon. At first it had irked him no end to hear the *ping!* of a WhatsApp message being deposited to her phone late at night, sometimes even after they had made love. Often, while trying to fall asleep, he could hear her clicking away on her phone keyboard. After a while he learned to ignore it, but he still felt a twinge of jealousy to hear her giggling at whatever little jokes she shared with Savalon. Other times, after he had pulled in for the night, tired from his students and his meetings (he was now chair of the Cultural Studies Unit and so had more demands on his time), her Facebook Messenger would ring, and if she had stayed up to read a book, she might take the phone outside to chat with Savalon. Even though Savalon was a gay man, Dexter felt there was still something off about his woman, and now his wife, having middle-of-the-night discourses with another man. He wondered, didn't Savalon have anyone lying next to him? Why was he messaging her at such off hours? And then he realized what it was that was truly bothering him: he did not feel respected by this other man. Men — real men, straight men — understood these boundaries. But this bullerman apparently did not.

That aside, the couple seemed to be making strides in their married life and their careers. Jacqueline had landed a tenure-track job in the Women's Studies Unit at the university where Dexter taught. They bought a nice house in an upscale gated community and immediately adopted two puppies from the RSPCA. One of their hobbies was cooking together, and it had even become a little competitive, with Dexter wanting to outdo Jacqueline in the gourmet department. They took to posting their latest successes on Instagram, then waited to see which one of their friends and acquaintances would weigh in and who would get the most likes.

An election year arrived on the island, and five of Dexter's former schoolmates ran as candidates in local constituencies, each of them winning their seat. The following year, as their party soared to power in general elections, three of these representatives were selected to head government ministries, including Benton Anthropode, the new minister of communications. He called Dexter shortly after his swearing-in to ask if he would be interested in a contractual position as a speech writer, especially to craft the monthly addresses to the nation that the prime minister gave. Dexter was well aware that the PM was taking a beating in the press and on social media for his lacklustre discourses. He also knew that many of the party faithful were semi-illiterate, poor people who had little to hope for and continued looking for a charismatic leader who would tell them what to do, how to think. Little had changed in the country since plantation days, as he would often bemoan to Jacqueline, his students, whoever was listening. He decided to take the job. The money Bentie offered was certainly a bonus.

Within a few months, people were soundly praising the PM's speeches. Journalists waxed enthusiastic how he was now "speaking the language of the people" and "not mincing any words" in his addresses. Dexter was pleased. He was especially pleased with an oft-quoted line from the PM's May address: "You may have come from the barrack yard, but that doesn't mean you are mentally enslaved! When you enrich others, abundance shall be yours!" Critics charged that the intent of the PM's words was exactly *to* keep poor people enslaved, working pointlessly for the wealthy elite on the island, vainly hoping that they, too, could one day achieve prosperity. Dexter knew the power of words; he also knew that true equality in the society was an impossibility. The masses lapped it up, the polls showed an even greater following for the party, and with the money Dexter was earning, he and Jacqueline built an Olympic-size pool on their property. This was followed by the purchase of a fully loaded cabin cruiser. With Dexter's new political recognition came additional perks: endless invitations to social events, dinners, fundraisers, fêtes. At first, Dexter would take Jacqueline along with him, but after a while she began to decline these invitations.

Jacqueline was becoming more involved in the feminist and queer activism instigated by her colleagues in the Women's Studies Unit. They were at the forefront of newly public demonstrations calling for changes to laws that criminalized same-sex relationships. The party in power — Dexter's cronies — were adamantly opposed to changing the legislation. There were ministers who openly scorned LGBTQ+ people and used words in parliament like *battyman* and *lesbo*. Dexter noticed that the more Jacqueline became immersed in her activism, the more her communications with Savalon increased. Savalon had recently spearheaded a successful campaign to strike buggery laws off the books in Trinidad and Tobago, where he was based. Jacqueline informed Dexter that together, she and Savalon were organizing a queer rights conference at the university, and Savalon had been invited as the keynote speaker.

Two weeks prior to the conference, Dexter walked through the door to discover Jacqueline with a new haircut. The sides of her head were shaved, and a long forelock of curly hair was hanging down over her left eyebrow.

"*What have you done?*" He was livid.

Jacqueline fixed her gaze on him. Things had been tense in their house for some time. She knew Dexter was annoyed with her new activities, but she was equally annoyed with his. Neither had been speaking to the other about these annoyances — only cold silences and tight lips. They had basically been leading separate lives for the past three months.

"Wha'appen?" She slipped into the local creole. Dexter had been noticing more and more of this lately. "It wouldn't *suit* yuh party people?" She was vex, he could tell.

He felt he didn't even recognize this person as the woman he had married — and it wasn't just the new haircut. "Oh, you trying to look like one of *them*?" he sneered. "You and your buller crew, your precious battyboy Savalon?"

She looked at him long and hard. Then she said, "He is going to be my new dean soon."

Dexter didn't know how to take that news. Did she mean that Savalon was going to be her superior, so she had been currying favour with him all these weeks because she saw the writing on the wall? Did she mean that she was letting Dexter know he had better start respecting Savalon, because now this "battyboy" would be her new boss? *His* new boss? That Dexter would have to answer *to him*?

●

LEAVING HIM IN STUNNED SILENCE, JACQUELINE EXITED THE house and went to that night's demonstration. A wealthy local White woman who enjoyed wearing masculine drag had been thrown out of La Spirulina, the restaurant of one of the tourist hotels, when she tried to use the men's restroom. A crew from the Women's Studies Unit plus local LGBTQ+ groups were all coming out to protest the discriminatory act. They held signs proclaiming *Womyn have the right to be whoever they want to be!* and *Gender Discrimination!!!*

Earlier that day, in a poorer part of the island, Teresa Beckett, mother of three, was murdered by her estranged husband, against whom she had taken out a restraining order the week before. Teresa's husband chopped her body up and placed the pieces into two pigtail buckets. Her head, however, had not been found. On the way home from the demonstration, Jacqueline was dropping her work colleagues off when they heard the news come over the car radio. There was silence. Then someone offered, "So much of these women getting killed by these damn men, eh? I glad ah does stay de *fock* away from dem!"

"Gyal, dat is de *troot!*"

Jacqueline said nothing. She didn't know who Teresa Beckett was, but she thought of those three children who were now motherless. Of the murderous man who was still at large. She couldn't help it, but a picture of a jaggedly sawed-off head, eyes rolled white, flashed through her mind, and she felt vomit rise up in her throat. What the *fuck*. Nausea turned to anger, to venom.

Jacqueline drove home, scanning through the stations on the car radio, hoping to find some update about the murder. She knew there would be no demonstration for Teresa Beckett, no placards, no outpouring of public rage and grief. More likely, people would blame the victim on social media: Why she stay wit de man if she knew he was a killer? Why she didn't leave him sooner? Why she didn't tek she tree pickney and *run*? Even: She mussa like dat big prick too much to leave.

Jacqueline also knew that her group of colleagues and activist friends would not be protesting Teresa's gruesome murder. Not today, not tomorrow — never.

The queer rights conference was a big success, and Savalon's keynote address was well-received, with excerpts printed in all the local papers. His impassioned cry for legalizing same-sex relationships in the country created a stir not only amongst the upper echelon of society (many of whom were closeted LGBTQ+ people themselves) but also amongst some members of the opposition party. Word had gotten around that Savalon was poised to take over as dean of social sciences at the university, and so some members of the opposition party began to woo him into joining their camp.

Before he flew back to Trinidad, Savalon went for drinks with Jacqueline. He had spent a week after the conference checking out the new digs that would be provided by the university, as befitted a dean. Over the cheeky cocktails they had ordered at Scarlet, a trendy west-coast bar, Savalon gushed over the plans he had for the renovated nineteenth-century mansion overlooking the Gold Coast. "Pure Edra! Girl, I don't know *how* I'm going to do it, if I have to sell an arm, a leg, a spleen — I am *going* to have some fabulous furniture up in heah!" He tugged at his bamboo straw with his lips, slurping up his cocktail. "And the *walls* — Benjamin [clap] Moore [clap] First [clap] Light [clap]! You *know* that is going to turn some *heads!*"

Jacqueline smiled to herself. Same old Savalon. Nothing had really changed despite the degrees, the plum administrative positions, the media exposure, the activism. He was still the inflated character she had come to know and love back at Howard. Full of himself, but full of a love for life as well, a *joie de vivre*.

Savalon checked his phone. "Oh, hon, I got to *go*! Gotta get to that airport before the plane leaves without me!" He jumped up from the table.

Jacqueline had carried him to Scarlet in her car; she thought she was carrying him back to his hotel so he could collect his luggage and then she would drive him to the airport. "Don't you need a ride?" she asked.

"Oh, no, someone is coming to pick me up. I'll call you when I get in?" He leaned across the table and smooched her on both cheeks. "Bye! Later!"

Curious, Jacqueline waited a few moments after Savalon left, then made her way to the ladies' room, hoping to catch a glimpse of who had come to pick him up. She was not disappointed. In the parking lot, she saw Savalon get into a black Audi that looked awfully familiar. It was Benton Anthropode's car, and he was kissing Savalon full on the mouth in the front seat.

•

DEXTER SAT NUMBLY IN HIS OFFICE. HE HAD JUST ENDED A
phone call with his mother. His father had been diagnosed with
Alzheimer's. For months his father had been acting strangely —
putting the orange juice in the cupboard instead of the fridge, for-
getting common words midsentence, and seemingly confused by
ordinary routines, such as squeezing toothpaste onto a toothbrush.
Last week he had wandered out through the front gate of the house
in only his jockey shorts. Dexter knew his father had come from
humble beginnings — he was nothing of the intellectual giant that
his son had become. But still it bothered Dexter that his father's
mind was going.

Dexter went to the gilt-edged mirror that hung over a glass
shelf where he kept his Scotch and goblets. He wanted to see if his
cranium was finally respiring, throbbing, the way he had always
feared it would, exploding and leaking through his ears, all his
brilliance seeping away. *What if all of this is for naught?* He studied
his hairline, wondering how much of his father's DNA he had
really inherited. He turned to look at his books, those that held
pride of place between the two Black Power fists. Where there had
once been four books, there were now eight. *Even if my mind goes,
it will have been recorded for posterity.*

He poured himself a long drink. His mother would need his
help with his father now. He suddenly wondered if Jacqueline
would take care of him if he, one day, faced his father's same fate.
He and Jacqueline had drifted so far apart. He poured another
drink, and realized he was afraid to go home, to face his wife, her
coldness.

He had a deadline to submit another prime ministerial speech.
Dexter sat down in front of his computer, the bottle of Scotch at
his right, and began composing: "There are certainties we have
all become accustomed to in life. But sometimes life seems full of

uncertainties. My people, rest assured that I, as your leader, have a firm hand on the helm of this ship. Do not become perturbed and enervated by the vicissitudes of life, but trust in those with the intellect and the fortitude to lead you from darkness into light."

How to Build a Saddis

Step One

Marvin was een Miss Angie parlour playing arcade game *Street Fighter*, when Satan grab he up, all ten years of frame he had, an carry he outside, an een front of everyone — elders, big woman, odder children, teenage gyals, gunmen, everybody — pantsed he right dey, Marvin lil brown behind exposed een de streetlamp for all an sundry to see. No one knew what possess Satan dat night to try ting so, 'cause he had about six or seven years on Marvin. Marvin wasn't taken *dat*, small as he was. He crept up de hill an went een de yard overlooking de hole where Satan an de odder monsters would lime, smoking weed, drinking puncheon, laughing, joking an playing a game of wapee. Quietly, he line up a setta bottle an big stone on de wall overlooking de hole, an den he juss bade dem down *good*, an dey trew back dey heads, shouting, wondering what imps had just pelt dem.

Satan made he out, bawlin, "Yuh muddercunt! Yuh ban from de hill!" to which Marvin responded, "Oh ho? Is who banning me?" an cheupsed loudly. Den, "Ah bringing meh cutlass fuh yuh!"

Young saddis was gone, dey could never ketch he, he was too fass an too sly. He really did go home an took out he granfadda cutlass, an, mounted by Ogun, eyes red, he went back up de hill, determined to right de wrong, to *deal* wit dem once an for all! He pass he granfadda een de yard like a full bus, grabbed de tree line, an kept walkin. He granfadda fuss watch Marvin, he lil stone face, manoeuvring up de hill wit a cutlass almost as big as he was, an den de ole man took off at once een hot pursuit, bawlin "Emma!" — de name of he dawta an Marvin mudda — to come an stop she chile from committing murder. By de time dey caught up wit Marvin he was already swinging at Satan een front de arcade. Satan had pull he cutlass as well, an de two danced, everyone holing dey bret. It was all granfadda an mudda could do to wrest dat cutlass from Marvin small han. Marvin would have none of it, an it was only wit much effort, an cole water dash pon he head, dat dey finally calm he. An is so saddis started he journey, building up he courage an resolve an resistance, until by age twelve he was pure iron.

Step Two

Saddis lived behind he darkers. Bare back, one foot cock up on de light pole, morning noon night, blazing sun, rain, break-a-dawn dew, he dey. Steeling heself for de war to come. A souljah, waiting on a command, a leader, a cause dat never came. He started hustlin from form two, age twelve, a lil weed, some rocks, taxing chirren een de hallways at school. School was a trial, a burden. Reading hut he head; trying to focus on de words of a page give he terrible headaches. From teachers it was just licks licks an more licks, an "Yuh duncey!" "Yuh chupid!" Some days dey was no money to travel to de school which was far far from he home. No one had tawt to build a high school een he area, an de nearest one was already full. He had was to go to one on de odder side of town. Some days dey was no shoes eider; he cousin would pass an tief dem to walk down de hill to catch a P car to he job een de city. Marvin couldn't go to school een a ketchass slippers an so he was home fuh de day, playin video game an smokin weed.

Step Three

Saddis would go to school or break biche during de weekdays, when everyone else een de househole was at wuk or school, but nights an weekends was anodda scene. Den home was quarrel, fight, stab up, brick to head, planass. Home was he sisters runnin een an out de house een all kinda undress, getting into cars wit older fellas, sometimes big men, an coming back wit brands, a cellphone, dey nails an hair done. Home was he stepfadda bussin he mudda lip an he havin to jump een an defend it. He would pull an pull on de weed, sometimes sneak a lil puncheon from he granfadda if he could, just to drown it all out. Loud loud music to cancel out de shoutin an cussin, de dishes breakin, de dogs barkin. He would imagine pulling a gun an holing it to he stepfadda's head, for once gettin he to shut up, for once seeing he pee he pants an beg de way he heard he mudda begging when dey would get way.

Step Three (B)

Early o'clock Marvin learned dat school was as unsafe as home an de streets. At a tender age a bigger, stronger boy had push he in de cubicle in de boys toilet an tried to pants he an interfere wit he in ways he had been warned about by he mudda. He fought, he screamed, but de boy was so much bigger an stronger. All dis added to de rage he already felt. He couldna tell de teacher because he knew de teacher would nah even care. He also knew if word got out dat anudda boy had touch he, he woulda get call bulla man, an dat he could never live down. So saddis buried it, deep, an it smouldered an stormed inside he, de iron een he soul tunnin to steel.

Step Four

From small Marvin had watched de Men een Black mount de hill, racing tru de squeeze-up narrow streets in vans, sometimes masked down wit bulletproof, terrifying een dey powers. He had seen dem kidnap man who later "disappeared," had seen dem buss down doors, make grannies scream, had seen dem beat ole men for no reason odder dan it gave dem a hard-on. When Marvin's tun came he took it like a man, fuss de cuff to face, den de boot to he side as he lay on de ground wit he bredrens, hans on he head, a normal day for de Men een Black, harassing yutes an searching for whatever dey could find een de pockets of tree quarters, an if dey couldn't find anyting maybe planting a lil coke to cover a quota back at de station. Saddis grew accustom to dem, never re-sisting de steady jamming. Sometimes he would get small lock up, fingerprinted, shoved een a filtee cell wit odder yutes like heself, while dey waited out de seventy-two hours, an when no charges could stick dey would let he go. Once, a particular officer started tracking he, found Marvin number from de arrest sheet, an started calling he, talking about "When ah could see yuh tuh suck dat long prick?" Saddis responded wit "Watch nuh, if you ever call dis phone again is you an yuh mudda an yuh sister go end up een a *big* grave, yuh hear?"

Step Five

By fifteen saddis decided it made more sense to be on de Block dan stay een school, take licks, be bored, be suspended, get into fights, or be de class clown. Being on de Block meant he could get he own pair of Jordans, a nice gole chain. He could rock brands, look good, smell good. He also wanted a pipe to hole at he waist, so dat if anyone — *anyone* — were to step to he again een life he could deal wit dem swiftly.

"Daaawg, wais dat one? Wais dat one?" Jaleel was coming up short again an beggin favour an Marvin didn't want none of it. He had already trusted Jaleel close to tree hundred dollars een rocks an he was fed up wit dis.

"Look rock so, nah? Move from by me! You owin me tree. Dohn come round here until yuh have it!" An Marvin flicked de end of he cigarette into de dark, moving he tall lanky frame from under de street light. Jaleel evaporated into de darkness, a hunched, dejected figure.

Marvin went inside de building. He didn't really like being inside, but he had to disappear long enough to make sure Jaleel didn't come back an try beg again. De stairwell was dim, but Marvin could make out he boy Skins leaning back in a chair, he legs open an a woman's head between dem. "Dawg, yuh want some ah dis? Is free wet head tonight."

De woman raise she head for a minute an Marvin saw she was White. He tawt, *de West? Fairways?* He tawt she looked like de

woman dat read de news on TV. Rich people. An here she was
sucking he boy's piggy een a stairwell on Nelson Street.

"Nah, ah good."

He went up de stairs.

Step Six

Marvin was relieved to find dey was no one on de roof. He could
smoke he weed een peace, contemplate de city from dese heights.
Sex an women were no release fuh saddis. He tawt, *Yuh nevah
know if a gyal is a trap. Setting you up to tief your money, to have
you killed. Yuh nevah know if she have a nex man, plenty man, a
chile fadda, a disease. Why bodda!* He tawt, *Betta to get a wet head
now an again from some halfway decent gyal an keep to yuhself. Steel
yuhself for de war. Keep yuh iron close een yuh pants. Never let your
guard down, never take a chance.*

Still de young gyals used to come round Marvin, but instead
of tracking dem he tried to school dem. Chirren having chirren,
yet still dey would push up dey young chesses an bend over for he,
squat down, dancing, twitching, making dey backsides jump wit
any rhythm dat hovered een de air: car stereos, speaker from a window, de big music trucks at Carnival time. Dey would come round
Marvin looking for love, or money, looking to be bred by he, trap
he een love an money, as dey had been taught by dey muddas. But
Marvin didn't get tie up, he stayed like a fadda figure to dem. But
still dey even wanted to tackle *dat*, de fadda figure, an *dat* was a
whole ugly story, a heap of bacchanal going back an back to slavery
days an barrack yard. Saddis lef it *alone*.

Step Seven

De False God kept all de boys on de Block paid. It was he running de drugs game while posing off as de saviour of de poor. If
you do my bidding is money. Pray five times a day. Learn to read
de Koran. Wear a muklah, go to jumma. Dis haram, dat haram.
Marvin fell een, den out, of de rituals. Fuss it felt good, but having
to pray before goin robbin an killin just didn't make sense. Saddis
didn't know which set of bandits to fall een wit. De False God had
he following plenty rules, but De Party was jus dat self — *party
time!* Now that he was old enough to vote, de campaigners took
a new interest een he. Election season he could bote eat a food an
fête: *party!* De music truck, rum an roti sharin: *party!* De party
campaign soca songs to put you een a trance wit dey Spiritual
Baptist rhythms, endless *party!* Carefully choreographed dance
moves, cocoyea brooms to sweeeeep away all de evilness een de
lan, an red-pantied, big-bottom women: *party!*

Marvin was young but he was not dumb. He took de campaign
T-shirts wit de money tucked inside, signed up for de ghost wuk
gangs, an collected several cheques under multiple names every
fortnight, but he saw tru all de lies an de mamaguy. Survival.
Politicians an dem didn't come from where he came from. Dey
didn't know what it was to have to walk up an down a steep hill
for your whole life, to have no current an no water, to bade een
stanpipe, to face empty cupboards an a empty fridge. Saddis side-
stepped the cult of the party, evaded de tumb of de False God.
There were no leaders.

Step Eight

Before he went on a wuk Marvin used to fast. Fast an pray. Used
to push heself to de point of anger, anger at all those who had

it easy een life, all dose who felt because dey had it easy een life somehow meant dey were betta dan he. De ones who watch he cut eye; de gyals who squeeze up deyself passing he on de pavement or bunch up deyself small small small een de back seat of a taxi, de bank workers and shop gyals, fraid to touch he, scrunching up dey face as if dey smelling shit. He would starve heself until he anger an he hunger bun togedda, until he had no heart, an it was easy to pull a gun on someone an stick it een dey jaw or ress it against dey forehead an watch dey shit deyself while he boys ramfled tru pockets, drawers, cupboards, purses. De first time Marvin hole a gun een he han he was nine; he liked de weight an de coolness of it, an by fifteen it an weed were he bess frens.

Saddis had terrible headaches an terrible nightmares, an sometimes jumbie visions dat invaded he head, unwelcome scenes of ripping men apart wit a knife, chopping off a man head an flinging it far an wide, shooting up multiple people all at once wit a big machine, cutting up saddises wit a tree line, limb from limb. Sometimes Marvin cried quiet quiet een he room, dark like de grave, while he mudda pace de floor above he, four o'clock een de morning, ketchin she powers. De whole yard was rank wit obeah. Obeah from badmind neighbours, from family who wanted de lan, from de odda child muddas of he absent fadda, from wicked envious people at he mudda's wukplace.

Marvin hated de visions an secretly wondered if he was really a demon. But he tole no one, just put on he darkers an rested heself on de Block. He went on more scenes wit he boys. He watched he bredren — fellas he had born an grown up wit — end up een body bags, especially de ones carrying so much man ghost it was a surety dey woulda end up een de cemetery, all dat baggage weighing dem down.

Somehow Marvin managed to dance between bullets. One time a saddis cock a gun right at he head an pull de trigger, an de gun jam. He had been giving de saddis a whole setta robber talk before it happen, like he really wasn't afraid to die, like maybe death would have been some kind of relief. But de gun stuck an he had to live to see anodda day.

By de time Marvin reach twenty-tree he noticed de young fellas coming up were moving *different*. Dey didn't care who dey touch — gyal, granny, even baby. Marvin felt sick. He had no problem holing a gun to a big man head, makin man bawl fuh he life — especially if de saddis was no saint an had probably done the same to odder men — dey all een de life, so it go. But *dese* monsters — mad! Why distress de elders, gyal, babies? What de fock?

Saddis became even more watchful. One day a yute just saunter up to he as Marvin was bracing de telephone pole, one foot cock up, bareback, de usual darkers on even though it was midnight, he nines rolled up een he sliders so even babylon couldna mek it out, an de yute just bawl at he, "Yow, saddis, yuh had any papers?"

Marvin, who was already smoking, blank he an continue smoking. He was busy watching a night star shining above de electricity wire, to de right of de moon.

De yuteman, vex now, tried again: "Saddis! Wha'appen? Like you gone tru?"

Marvin very slowly tun he head an watch yuteman dead een he eye. He just stare he down until de yuteman caught a chill an move off, mumbling, "Mad muddercunt!"

Times got harder on de Block. Marvin was braced by Kwesi, whom he had known since boyhood days. "Dey lookin for a team to kidnap dis woman. Some big ranker wife. Me ent know wha she do im but yuh could mek big money if yuh want een."

Marvin didn't even hesitate. "Nah, man. Dais not my scene. bredrin! I not on *dat*."

Kwesi watched Marvin. To he Marvin had a heart of stone, not quite a monster but capable of monster antics. "Wha'appen, yuh fraid de charge?"

"No. What ah hurtin dis woman for? What she ever do me? Yuh know?"

Kwesi got quiet. He remembered a time he had gone on a wuk, an two maddy yutes ridin wit dem. When dey reach een de people house it had two young dawtas, in dey nighties, line up, terrified. While he an de odders were tyin up de family an taping dey mouts, one a de yutes took one a de gyal een a room an rape she. Kwesi had done nuttin. He ignored de gyal screams, de pleadin, de beggin, while dey ransack de house. Den all en a sudden it got rell quiet. Yuteman came out de room, an dey left. He never found out what happened to de gyal.

You have now completed your saddis. Congratulations!

Alone een he room, lyin on a mattress on de floor, Marvin wrapped up een a sheet like a cocoon, evading de mosquitos an cockroaches, swaddling heself. He felt safe, like no one could touch he or penetrate he, een he own personal womb. He rocked he foot slow at fuss, den fass fass, rocking heself to sleep. He dreamt, horrible scenes of bloodshed, severed fingers, a knife plunging again an again into some man chess. He didn't know if he was de murderer or if he was just watching de murders. But he knew he had to watch he own back an not get kill, even een dis dream, dis dream above all, because of ancient debts still owing.

Yellow Dog Blues

It doesn't matter now. Now I can just watch from afar, I don't have to worry, to wait; I don't have to drink or eat last. I can just watch. Or not watch. Just now the little Blackies will join me here, I know. I saw one of them eat some too-old meat from a can last night, so likely her belly will run, and, well, the other one, ole Grey Muzzle, I dream (yes, even here I can dream; isn't it strange?), I dream he get bounce down by a car on Saddle Road. There's only the pups left now and they will have to make out, but garbage is plentiful in these parts. (I remember overhearing a woman complaining one day about how people are so *stink*, and then watching me with pity in her eyes.) The Blackies and I used to roam all in the back of Santa Cruz. I had been on my own for some time after fleeing my humans, and then I spotted the Blackies down by the river and I just started to shadow them from a distance. We were never like family — it is impossible with us and the pecking order that we have — but they allowed me to sort of run with them (behind them, really) and whatever they left behind after eating, I would clean up. We roamed like this for a good while, until ... well ... until I left. I was always a loner, so I don't even know if they missed me or even noticed that I was gone. It was hunger that kept us routing, day and sometimes night too, until the pads in my paws were so sore, and sometimes they even felt burnt from the hot hot pavement, but we had to keep routing. The burning hunger for survival in our bellies had us moving from garbage bin to garbage bin, sneaking into people's yards to see if they had put out some leftovers or accidently dropped some consumables. Sometimes we even chased chickens or ducks (unskillfully and unsuccessfully), and once one of the Blackies found an egg and mashed that up quick quick. We were in constant hunger and thirst, sometimes in pain as well. The one thing we shared was a fear of humans. Some of us knew more about the true nature of humans than others. But more about that later.

One night as we were routing, we saw some kind of spectre at the street corner, near to where the goats lived. I could smell the smell from far, and wondered what caused it, but when we came across this wretched being, I had no doubt the smell was coming from him. Putrid, rotting flesh. The dog could not have been very old at all, but he already looked completely worn down by life, and the smell ... He could barely raise his head, but when he did I saw that maggots had eaten away half his face. The chain dangling down from him and into the drain told me that someone had dragged him and left him there at the street corner to die. He was struggling to stay on his four feet, to stay upright, to stay alive. For what? Was he waiting vainly in the hopes that the same humans who had dragged him there would return to collect him? We crossed the road quickly, me and the Blackies. There was nothing to gain from him. Truth was, he was simply rotting before our eyes, on that street corner, in the middle of the night, with the sensation of live worms eating away his face.

On the whole, I like the smell of carrion, but not when it comes from one of us. *Eau de* rotting bird is probably my fave, and a good roll in a rotting carcass does wonders for hiding my scent and allowing me to traverse strange territories unassailed. But you have to find exactly the right bird — not just any one will do. The other day I came across a choice piece. The Blackies were busy in the garbage anyways, and so I helped myself to a good rubdown. I was in front of the Rottweiler Kingdom yard — I call it that because I saw these dogs so well cared for that I figured they must be ruling their humans and not the other way around. But the joke was on them: they were imprisoned. I never, ever saw them leave that yard. They did not even go for any walks on a leash (which, admittedly, was not any kind of real freedom, was it?). Whereas I was free. Yes, okay, free to starve, to rout, free to have no shelter, but also free to roll in my choice of carrion without some stupid human telling me *no* and *stop* and *ewww*. I took my time, slowly lowering my bony frame onto that squished, festering mockingbird. The Rotts were silent, as their breed is apt to be; their nine pairs of eyes just watched me. They are very stealthy. When I was done, I slowly got up (okay, this time I was not making style, but really and truly my bones were feeling old and a bit of arthritis was setting in), shook myself off gruffly, and stepped away with pride. They? They could only *watch*.

Mrs. Blackie is going to have another litter of pups soon. Mr. Blackie cannot resist her when she is in heat, and maybe that's why they have been routing together for so long. Then again, they could be brother and sister. These kinds of things do happen. They actually resemble each other, so there is a good chance. I have seen Mrs. Blackie birth four litters. The pups rarely survive. Some are run over by cars, some die from disease and malnutrition, and others end up like that poor chap we ran into on the street corner. For a while one of the grown pups did rout with us, but one day he was gone and I never found out why. You learn not to get attached to your pack mates. You learn to remain aloof. Death is imminent, often sudden and unexpected. Better not to know, I always say.

A bitch in heat does nothing for me. I did once have a human family, and I was castrated at a young age. I would just wait until Mr. and Mrs. Blackie finished their tie and off we would go again. Sometimes their constant humping when she was in heat cramped my style. But whatever. It was still better and safer for me to travel with them than alone.

My earliest memory is of being flung out of a moving car, not too far from where our hunting grounds now are. There is a long stretch of bush and abandoned cocoa plantations, and this is where the human who had my mom decided to get rid of her — and us. I remember crawling out of a cardboard box that had busted open from the impact of hitting the ground. It was pitch black, so my siblings and I just started to cry because we were so scared. Where was Mom? We whimpered and cried for a good while until Mom finally did show up, limping and frantic and scared as much as we were. She licked us all over, but was obviously in pain. Once she knew she had all of us together, she tried her best to lie down and nurse us, although she could not get comfortable due to her injury.

We hid in the bush like this for a while, until one day Mom came back attached by a rope to some humans. They carefully put us into another cardboard box. We all went to a place with lots of dogs in cages. There were cold tiles and bright lights and a sharp smell that made me sneeze. We lived there for a while in a kennel. Mom ate so much her milk started gushing for us and we were all ecstatic! Her leg healed, and I remember getting poked a few times with a needle. It was just hard sometimes listening to the other dogs around us who were crying and crying and crying, even howling — because they were scared, because they were lonely, some because they missed their humans.

Different people started to come to look at us, pick us up, pet us, play with us. Mom wasn't too keen about it, but there was little she could do. A man and a woman and a child came one day. The woman picked me up and made a lot of cooing sounds and then placed me in the arms of her daughter. The man just watched. The little girl hugged me close to her heart — I could feel it beating fast, she was so excited — and then she buried her face in my neck and kissed me. I was so happy I started licking her face, thrilled to have such an innocent human this close to me. I could feel the love pouring out of her, and all I wanted to do was reciprocate! I left my mom and siblings that day.

The family that took me in were very good to me, I must say. I mean, the man wasn't too thrilled with me, I could tell, but from time to time he would pat me on the head and say, "Good boy." The woman would get upset if I peed or pooped on her tiled floors, but otherwise she also showed me some affection, sometimes gave me a toy or a treat. But I lived for Talia. I knew it was her name because her mom called her "Taaaaaa-liiiii-aaaaaaaaa" the same way that Talia would call me "Saaaaaaaaaa-nnnnnndyyyy!" She named me Sandy because of the yellowish colour of my fur. She was my world, from the time she showed up that day to take me home until the day she disappeared.

I don't know exactly what happened. I used to sit by the gate every day, waiting on the sound of the car that would bring Talia home from school. I knew the sound of the engine, I knew the type of music the driver played — I knew everything about that car: its smell, how fast its wheels spun. That day the car never came. I waited still and then the woman showed up. She jumped out of her car and came running through the gate — didn't even remember to close it after her — and ran into the house. I tried to follow her, to get her attention, but she completely ignored me while she breathlessly and excitedly talked with her hand next to her face even though no one else was there except me. She did this for a long time. I sat a little distance off, quietly watching her, but more watching the gate and the road, looking out for Talia. The man showed up. He, too, jumped out of his car and ran into the house. He grabbed the woman and she started crying, loudly. He tried to comfort her but she was distraught. I felt scared, worried. Where was Talia?

I went outside to the gate, which was still wide open. I cautiously poked my nose outside, sniffing, trying to see if I could smell Talia. Nothing. I went to my doghouse and picked up the stuffed toy Talia had given me that morning before she left for school. It still had her scent on it. I lay down on my bed, the toy between my paws. It got darker and darker. I could hear the man and woman shouting in the house, the woman still crying. A van with flashing blue lights pulled up at the gate. I jumped up, barking. The gate was still open and these humans could just walk in. I went running to the gate and the men who came out of the van stopped. The man and the woman came running out of the house, the man grabbing me roughly by my collar. He chained me up by my doghouse. Everyone went inside. I waited. My stomach started to growl.

I stayed chained up like that for three days. Many people were coming in and out of the house; at one point someone noticed me and gave me some water to drink. The man came and gave me a bowl of dog chow on the second day, which I wolfed down hungrily. I had no choice but to pee and poop where I was. Nobody noticed or cared. I could smell the sadness and the fear coming off all the humans that passed through the gate. It seemed the woman never stopped crying.

Talia never came through the gate again. With every day that she was gone I got sadder and sadder.

The man and the woman barely looked at me after that. It was as if they hated me — for what, I did not know. Once in a while I whimpered, especially if they forgot to feed me, which happened more and more, and the man would shout at me angrily. "Shut up! Just shut up!"

One day the woman got in her car and drove away and never came back. After that I stayed chained up for a week, with no food and no water. A neighbour noticed me, talked to me, and tried to talk to the man, who didn't want to come out of the house. The neighbour started feeding me and giving me water over the fence. One night she climbed over the fence, unchained me, and then opened the side gate so that I could leave. I did just that. I wanted to go looking for Talia.

I was feeling pretty weak but I had seen enough dogs tear open garbage bags to know that I could probably find something to eat in them, so I ran until I found some smelly bags and then set to busting them, and I overturned any bins I could find. I spent the night eating a smorgasbord of human food I had never smelled or eaten before. It was kind of exciting, especially after hardly eating for weeks, but after a while I could feel my belly cramping and then I had some diarrhea. I was exhausted. Where to sleep? Between two buildings I found space that was dark and quiet and where I felt no human would disturb me. I curled up there on a piece of cardboard and tried to sleep. I dreamt of Talia.

And so I lived like this for quite some time, until I found the Blackies down by the river.

Life on the streets took its toll. I knew I looked a lot older than I was. I had some scars on my body from the many times humans threw rocks at us to drive us away from the garbage. Luckily, the injuries were all in places that I could lick and keep clean — if they had been on my face, I could have ended up like the dog at the crossroads, with flies laying eggs in my wounds and maggots eating my flesh.

I still looked out for Talia, but her scent had faded from my memory. If I ever came across her or anything of her again, I would know it, I would be overjoyed — but my life had become about finding food.

I remember the day a particular group of boys started pelting bottles and rocks after us, idle and stupid, being cruel for no other reason than it made then feel powerful. One of the boys was bigger than the others, and he had a big round head and bulging eyes. I saw him staring at me. I sensed there was something wrong with him. He didn't seem quite like the others. I didn't like him, so I barked twice at him and then quickly trotted away. Generally, I am a quiet dog, but this time I just *had* to say something.

Not long after this incident, I saw the same boy trying to catch a chicken. He had a big piece of wood and was just beating to death any chicken he could corner. There was blood and feathers everywhere. A man noticed what he was doing and yelled at him to stop. "That's not how you kill chickens!" he said. The big head boy stood there with his bloody club, like he didn't know what to say. He picked up one of the dead, shapeless chickens, put it in a sack, and walked up the road.

Anytime I saw him after this I would bark, turn, and run the other way. But one night I followed the Blackies into a yard — it smelled like someone had actually left some cooked food out for us. There were humans who saw us in need and didn't think anything of dishing out their leftover rice or chicken bones or macaroni pie onto some enamel plates and leaving these out in the yard for us to scavenge. These people were lifesavers to us. But you never knew who really were the kind ones and who might have left poisoned food out, because there were those kinds of humans too. You just never knew. You had to always have your guard up.

That night in the strange yard, we found some bowls of leftover pelau and dumpling waiting for us. I was so busy eating that I didn't notice when the box dropped over me from above. I was in pitch blackness, confused, not sure what was happening. I knew the Blackies were gone. They would have fled immediately.

I stood there, not making a move. I have never been an aggressive dog, so fighting was not my first instinct.

Suddenly, the box came off and I was blinded by bright lights. I felt hands grab me and a rope being tied around my neck and my legs. I tried to fight, but whoever was tying me was very strong.

It was the big head boy.

I started to bite him, and he yelled, "Ow!!" and then started beating me in my face with his fists and kicking me. I couldn't run away, as my legs were now tied. He threw me in the box and dragged me away from the house into the bush.

The last thing I remember was gasping to breathe after he tied the plastic bag around my head. Thankfully, I was losing consciousness when he poured the lighter fluid on me and set me on fire.

•

IT WAS A WOMAN WHO FOUND WHAT WAS LEFT OF ME THE next day. She covered her mouth in horror and ran away. Then others came to look, and another woman fell down on her knees and wept. People took pictures of my corpse, and these pictures went all over the world. Many, many people saw these pictures. From what I gather, so many people talked about what happened to me and were so upset about it that they made sure something would be done. I don't know what, if anything, will change, but I saw the big head boy taken away. One of those vans with the blue lights came and put him inside and drove off. I wonder if he went to the same place where Talia is.

Chupito's Last Stand

Back in jail. How was he going to get out of this one?

He didn't mean for things to have reached so far. He didn't mean to have fallen asleep. Now she knew everything.

And la Peruana would also find out. He would have to think fast. He believed la Peruana was still malleable, but with that Salvaje he would cut his losses.

Chupito fell asleep in the cell and woke to the *pss pss pss* of steam escaping the pressure cooker. Arroz con frijoles, moros y cristianos, Moors and Christians, the black beans and the white rice. His mother had gone into the backyard and brought back a hand of plantains and a hand of bananas; if they could find a little oil, they could eat tostones. The radio incessantly proclaimed,

"*Tic … tic … tic … bedeebeep bedeebeep!* Radio Reloj. La una cin-co minutos." There would be no meat again today, but that was all right. They would make do — maybe a little guava syrup would round the meal off nicely.

When he really woke up it was to the smell of man sweat, grime, dirty feet, and a weird puff of what smelled like marijuana. You could get anything in jail. Anything. The problem was that he was an outcast in here. Not Black enough to be part of the Jamaican crew, and not Latino enough to hang out with the Mara Salvatrucha 13 putos either. He kept to himself. Waited for the bell that would allow him to start calling the roster of women he had at his fingertips, calling, calling, calling collect, until someone, anyone, picked up. He would then recite his orders for each:

"Oye, mamita, call my father. Let him know that he needs to send me the money to pay the lawyer."

"I need you to come down on Thursday and deposit money in my account. Mami, I have nothing here. It is rats and roaches. Oh, and bring some photos of yourself, mami. You know the ones I like."

"I need you to go and see Julio and make that payment! I am *telling* you. Don't fuck it up!"

Chupito had probably been a pimp at some point in his life, but this was uncertain. What was known was that he had been a whore and had whored himself to both men and women from the age of twelve. Whaddya gonna do, papi? Havana was hopping with gringos, and Castro was pushing tourism like the latest drug. Las viejas flocked to him like nobody's business. He didn't mind a little wrinkled skin, a little sagging tetas. These bitches had the fulas, the money, baby! He used to tap his arm with his index finger to indicate his colour. "This," he would boast to anyone who would listen, "is like *gold*!" In truth, his skin was more of a reddish tone, red like the earth in the eastern provinces of Oriente, where his family had migrated from. But it drove las viejas wild, along with his chiselled physique, shown off in little more than some spandex trunks. He ate well while all around him people were frying up grapefruit-rind steaks and trying to find fifty culinary uses for banana peel.

In between the stories of his life, which he liked to fondly flip through like an old Rolodex, he remembered the attack from that Salvaje daughter of Ochun. She had fed him his plato fuerte, his main course, the standard midday Cuban meal which was meant to last a whole twenty-four hours if necessary — a leg of chicken, a hill of white rice, a peeled bañana, sliced tomatoes and cucumbers, and a triangle of guava paste with cream cheese. This was accompanied by a glass of Kool-Aid. But immediately after eating his meal, he had felt so sleepy he could not keep his eyes open. She had put something in his drink, he now realized. When he awoke from his impromptu nap, his gym bag was gone.

She had locked herself in the bathroom with it and found out everything he had been hiding from her for years. His phones. His wedding ring. Other women's credit cards. Keys to a Mercedes S-Class. Clothes she had never seen before, very expensive bespoke linens and fine silks. Keys to houses and fobs to condos (she assumed) that she knew nothing about.

When he tried to open the bathroom door, she waited a good while, laughing maniacally at him from inside, calling the numbers in his phones, talking to the women who answered. In his panic he began to break down the door, and that's when she picked up the wooden towel stand and attempted to beat him over the head with it. He tried to wrest it away from her, but his muscles were surprisingly flaccid, his grip impotent. He wondered if he would get an asthma attack (he had suffered from asthma since a child and he had nearly died on several occasions, his parents frantically rushing him to the Hospital Pediátrico Docente in Centro Habana in the middle of the night).

Chupito and Salvaje awkwardly danced their way out of the bathroom and into the living room; she screaming frantically, cussing him with every stink word in her vocabulary, a mixture of Trinidadian English and Cuban Spanish. "Puto! You fuckin' muddercunt pendejo! Malcriado, hijo de puta, is dead you go dead tonight, yuh stinkin comemierda!"

And somehow in this dance he used his very weight (he was a hefty 230 pounds, and although not very tall, was decidedly bulky) to push her down on the sofa. Pinning her, he wrapped his hands around her throat and carefully positioned his two thumbs directly over her windpipe. The thumbs hovered there, and she knew her life was also hovering before her, literally in this man's hands, this betrayer. And it was clearer than clear as a bell, as a freakin' solar flare, to her now: this *psychopath* — she needed to change the balance of power, and quickly. Over his right shoulder she saw the glass cabinet with all her Orichas, her santos, lined up and covered down in their silk and satin cloths, their numerous and carefully acquired adornments surrounding each of them, and she knew what she had to tell him. They were face to face, breath to breath, and she just whispered in his ear, "Oricha is watching!"

His eyes got suddenly big. He jumped off her. He felt confused, as if he were waking from a dream. What had he just done?

He stood in the middle of the room, astounded.

Salvaje was not finished with him yet. She went to Changó's cedar throne, the Oricha of thunder and justice, and grabbed his wooden sword, embellished with red and white beads, washed in omiero and the blood of two red roosters. Holding the sword aloft, she climbed on a chair. A keening cry came out of her mouth that was so otherworldly; Chupito's eyes grew even wider and he fell to his knees. "I beg your forgiveness!" he whimpered, not addressing Salvaje at all, but the manifestation of Changó, Kawo Kabiosile himself, who appeared before him now, brandishing the sword and looking quite ready to smite him dead with it.

Chupito ran out of there faster than a cat on its ninth life.

By the time he reached the metro station, the police were already waiting for him. They booked him on assault, as well as a number of other offences for which he had outstanding warrants. Not a first-time offender, and definitely "known to police," he went back to the city jail and waited. And plotted. How was he going to get out of this one?

The air in the jail was not good, unsurprisingly. At times he felt his chest tighten, and he asked the guards if he could get a puffer. They responded vaguely, and he figured he would have to recruit one of his women to bring the puffer for him. A delicate child, he had also suffered from numerous allergies. He told everyone that he was allergic to eggs and honey, but really these were spiritual taboos for him, as prescribed by his godmother, Eleana. She had warned him about Ochun, and especially daughters of Ochun, but he kept messing with her daughters, and kept catching hell because of it. Eggs and honey were sacred foods of Ochun's, so he was forbidden from consuming these. And yet, even these he at times could not resist — like the time that Salvaje had rubbed honey all over her body and her bollo — well, what was he to do?

He lay on his bunk and his mind went back to Cuba. His heyday on the Malecón, strutting his stuff for the yumas. And even before then: his childhood in Vedado before '89, before everything crumbled and the sky fell. Everything had started out nice. His papi had a party card and, as a young revolucionario, had assisted the peasants, teaching them how to read and write after the revolution, the great Campaña Nacional de Alfabetización of 1961. Chupito's mother had followed his father from the eastern provinces to worship at his feet, and to be his quasi-slave. She lived only for Chupito's father. Papi had moved his entire extended family from Oriente to the middle-class Havanese suburb of Vedado, with its wide streets and elegant boulevards, its art deco buildings and green spaces. All manner of brothers and sisters and cousins and nephews ended up in the spacious apartment on Línea. Life was good for a time, and

Chupito enjoyed the perks of having a father who worked in the government and had access to a multitude of things that ordinary Cubans did not. That was, until the Special Period hit, and then Chupito was suddenly and unceremoniously left to his own devices. He had spent his days wandering up and down Calle 23, from Paseo all the way to the Malecón and back, and saw what was taking place. He learned that rich, foreign White men had more dollars than rich, foreign White women, and that the vanity of foreign gay men was an easy mark..He cultivated his machismo in tight jeans which emphasized his butt crack (and oh, what a butt it was, mamita coñññooooo. The maricones went wild for him!). So he escorted his new gay friends to assorted activities and excursions, in and out of Havana — driving rented cars; going to the exclusive gay parties thrown by maricones con clout; playing tour guide, host, amigo; taking these new "friends" on beach excursions. Sometimes he got paid in fulas and sometimes he got more, like plane tickets to visit foreign countries, and life was good, ¡asere! To be young and fit and hot and Cuban was a beautiful thing, no? But success can make one overconfident — you could push your hand a little too far — and Chupito, being the only recognized son of his father and the apple of his mother's eye, had been raised without limits. So he gambled all and left Cuba for La Yuma, and that was the beginning of the end for Chupito.

The tata gave him a number of amulets to ensure that he would be protected in La Yuma, but his new post-menopausal White American wife, vain to the core (as was Chupito), in a fit of fury and rage, shoved the amulets down the garbage disposal one evening. She then hurled his Orichas down a flight of stairs, and poor Ellegua — lord of the crossroads, and all roads, the opener and closer of paths — shattered into a million pieces. And so Chupito's path also shattered into a million pieces. He began running helter-skelter all over the map of North America, with nowhere to rest his head. Through a series of further mishaps, he landed in Canada, and sought refuge in the Great White North. But here, too, his trials and tribulations persisted. Chupito did not know that Canadians — in defiance of U.S. policy on Cuba — refused to deport any criminally convicted person back to Cuba. And Chupito, who by this time only wanted to return to the bosom of his mami in Parraga, was stuck like glue to Canadian soil. No matter how many petty crimes he committed, he was undeportable. Perhaps it was the curse of Ellegua that returned him to an even more childlike state, in which his persistent desire was to suckle at the teta of his mami again and eat arroz con frijoles and ride his bicycle and just be, just be a young man full of revolutionary dreams and promise, just be a campesino like his mother's people and cultivate the red red earth and eat boniato and ñame and yucca from the earth that his wife would cook with garlic and olive oil, seasoned with cumin, and he would drink rum and beers with other campesinos, singing trova and boleros under the stars.

It was lights out now in the jail. He had made it through another day. He was strong, tougher than anyone knew. He came from people who had given the finger to the Americans, who had put their lives on the line, balls out, and aimed rocket launchers at Miami from in front of the Hotel Nacional. From people who had, even before that, fought off the Spanish with machetes, who had survived wars of independence and dictatorships and a revolution and the Special Period. He was not afraid. He yawned. Tomorrow he would make the round of calls again to all the women he could get to, whose minds he had tied up in his fingertips like fine spiderwebbing, and he knew — he *knew* — on some level that Salvaje would be expecting his visit. For a split second he thought, *But why should I go back there? She knows everything. She's the one who put me here.* But that thought was quickly submerged by an even bigger thought: *I will win.* And as he closed his eyes and snuggled down in his cot, he focused his thoughts intently on Salvaje's face, remotely hypnotizing her in her sleep.

●

BY THE TIME CHUPITO WAS RELEASED FROM JAIL, IT WAS AL-
ready October. La Peruana came to pick him up in the Mercedes —
he was hoping some of those monos comemierdas were watching
through the decrepit windows to see just how he had it, how he
was light years above these amateurs. When the two got back to
her condo, he quickly showered the stench of the jail off him, and
he didn't even bother to fuck her before he put on his best bespoke
clothes, a little Clive Christian cologne, Prada shoes soft as butter.
She was droning on about something, telling him how he needed
to change his ways if he wanted to be with her, that she was better
than all this jail shit, that her brother was *really* mad about him
making her stand bail, putting up her condo as collateral.

He barked at her suddenly. "Mami! I need some money if I am
going to get this business going again!"

She stopped midsentence, opened her mouth in astonishment,
stared at him, wrinkled up her face in disgust, and then flicked
her long, straight black hair several times in annoyance. Once that
momentary lapse was over, she resumed complaining about how
he needed to go to church more, all while she was opening her
Hermès wallet.

On the 401, Chupito was zooming in and out of lanes, pump-
ing Paulito FG on the stereo, already feeling extremely buzzed
and ecstatic from the six lines he had snorted before leaving la
Peruana's condo. He suddenly swerved across three lanes (causing
a few drivers to have mild heart attacks and serenade him with
a cacophony of horns) in a split-second decision to exit onto the
Allen Road. He needed to check up on Salvaje.

Driving down her tree-lined street, he could see the lights were
on in her third-floor bedroom window. He liked to imagine that
she had a man up there, right now, some negro no doubt, and then
imagine that he would wait outside until this man emerged, and

then imagine punching the life out of him. While he sat outside her house, he snorted a few bumps off his balled-up hand, actually hoping some pendejo would come out so that he could rush him in a coked-up rage of adrenalin, pummelling him. He noticed some big stones in her yard — these he would use to crush the man's head.

He dialed her number. He could actually hear her phone ringing from that open third-storey window. She didn't answer. He didn't leave a message. He began to dial another woman's number, then another's, Katerina, Lucy, la Flaca, la Peluosa ...

Day and night for the next seven days he passed by her house, sometimes stopping and watching, waiting, plotting; other times only driving by. He was never entirely sure she was there, as during the day the light in her window would not be on. She did not own a car, so he could not rely on that indicator. Sometimes he would phone her while he was outside her house; sometimes he would phone her when he was somewhere else, with someone else, often one of his other women.

One day, to his surprise, she picked up. "Hello?"

He didn't say anything. He wanted to have her off guard.

"Hello?"

Then, not wanting her to hang up, he said in a gruff and angry tone, "You never answer your phone."

There was silence. Then, "What do you want?"

"I want to come and see you. I missed you, mami. I want to explain."

"Explain what?"

"Well ... I know things got ... a little out of hand. But that's all in the past now. I'm a changed man. I want to make a fresh start. With you."

"With me?" She laughed. At first it sounded like a normal laugh. But as it tapered off, there was a hint of the maniacal.

"Yes." He could sound so sincere, so earnest. He had practised and practised. He knew he was such a good actor. It had paid off for him so many times.

"So … when do you want to see me?"

This was more than he had expected. She wasn't even putting up any resistance.

"I come tomorrow." He slipped out of his impeccable English for one brief moment.

"All right. Morning?"

Morning had always been their time. After he had dropped la Peruana off to work and before he visited one of the other women in his stable, later in the afternoon, right until it was time to pick up la Peruana at five o'clock, he would spend the mornings at Salvaje's, fucking, eating, and watching videos. She would complain and complain, but he always had an explanation as to why he could only be there at that certain time of day.

"Yes."

"Okay."

He felt secure now. He had his bases loaded. La Peruana, Salvaje, Katerina, Lucinda, la Flaca, la Peluosa … The latest addition, la Peluosa, always wanted to feed him and wash his clothes and shop online for him. He was considering giving her a baby on top of the pinga she already got, but he needed more time to ensure she wasn't a total loca like his ex-wife or something. The main thing was that he had calmed down Salvaje so that she would not do any more damage to his life. To their arrangement.

By 10:00 a.m. the next day, he was on her doorstep, freshly shaved, smelling of only a dab of cologne, wearing a designer track suit, his one diamond stud glittering in his ear. They had had their fallings-out before, and as far as Chupito was concerned, this was just another make-up-and-let's-get-on-with-it session. However, there had been times she was so mad she had withheld food. He wasn't sure if this was one of those times or not. But once he entered her house, he smelled the pollo asado and knew he was home free.

Later, after the sex and the video (*Memorias del Subdesarrollo* —
a classic), she went to check on the chicken. He dozed off, comfortable in her queen-size bed, not as luxurious or extravagant as the
king-size he shared with la Peruana, but still nice. It felt nice to be
back in it. All was right with the world.

Here she was with his plato fuerte. And a batido de plátano to
boot.

The chicken was so sweet and roasted to perfection that the
meat was falling off the bone. And the milkshake so thick the
straw could stand up in it. It was only a few minutes after he began
to eat that he felt his throat closing up, like a rock was stuck and
he couldn't swallow it down. Then his eyes were watering, his nose
running, and he suddenly felt so hot he threw the covers off. He
wanted to say something, but the rock in his throat wouldn't let
him. He looked up at her standing over him, her arms crossed,
observing him silently. He was now gesturing wildly to his throat,
thrashing his arms around, reaching for the phone. She moved
swiftly and suddenly to disconnect the phone from the wall jack,
then resumed her calm, distanced pose. She watched him without a sound, but as his eyes closed, he could hear that maniacal
laughter echoing through the tunnels of his mind as he tried to
follow the white light, a light burning, searing into his third eye.
At the last minute, the white light was snuffed out, and he found
himself falling, falling, feeling fainter now, the oxygen supply to
his brain cutting off. He spiralled, spiralling down, down into a
deep tunnel, and then he was following the darkness, an abysmal
hole of blackness, into a graveyard and a tomb like a prison, a
cage, with shackles and a big iron gate, carved into and under a
hillock, and so profoundly hidden in the cemetery. And he noticed
his clothes were already there, a complete outfit, a handmade silk
Apposta shirt, linen Armani trousers, and caramel Prada shoes,
all carefully laid out as if waiting for him, the clothes he had left
behind in the gym bag when he went to jail, and he knew that this

prison-tomb was so deep and dark and damp that no one would ever come to look for him there. *She did this*, he thought, before he flew over the clothes, into the clothes, and through the iron gates that locked up after him, as he lay down in the deep dank fetid cold wet black earth.

The Christmas House

Every year from Divali it would start. While other people were lighting deyas and eating curry off banana leaf, Hamza would be surveying his yard, assessing the project at hand. One year he power washed the whole house and yard, including the inside and out of the perimeter brick wall. When that was completed, he decided he would paint everything — the house, the perimeter brick wall, and the two gates (one for cars and one for pedestrians) — with a three-inch flat-cut brush. From mid-November until mere days before Christmas, the neighbours would see him outside each day, and sometimes into the evening, meticulously painting each metal rail in the gate, each brick-and-mortar line of the perimeter wall, the exterior walls and trim of the yellow house, the eavestroughs and drainpipes, the galvanized roof. Jericha, his common-law wife, would sit outside in a lawn chair each evening, watching him intently. Wherever he was painting, she would move the chair to be a few feet away from him, and would sit there, silently, watching his every move.

Another year he sold off all the ducks he had raised in a shed in the backyard and used the money to buy a roll of razor wire that he ran along the length of his perimeter wall, facing the squatter community where his pumpkin-vine in-laws lived. He bought new locks for the motorized front gate and installed security cameras in three locations on the property. He raised the perimeter wall by two rows of bricks. The in-laws had taken his brand new Navara van for a joy ride a week before, without his consent, and had returned it days later, mud splattered and with several dings in the bonnet. His common-law wife's family were always helping themselves to things in the yard: weed whackers, ladders, brooms, and rakes, any tools he might have left lying around. Since she had moved herself and her three children into his house (displacing his legitimate wife and children, the wife who had helped him build that house), it was as if he had no say or control over anything anymore. It was only when he got into his van every morning and headed out to check on the numerous businesses he had set up around the community that he got away from her clutches. She truly had him under heavy manners.

The year after the razor wire and security cameras, the massive decorations appeared. Beyond the blinking lights that Hamza would normally string around the edge of the roof and the front-facing windows of the house — pink and green and red, flashing, shimmering — he now added huge inflatable characters: an enormous white Santa Claus, a green Christmas tree, a black-and-white skating penguin, multiple snowmen, and, in addition, five gold wire-mesh angels. The Santa Claus was so big that the only place he could fit was on Hamza's roof, so up he went, secured by yellow nylon rope.

The villagers and Jericha's pumpkin-vine family had never seen anything like this. It was as if some winter wonderland had descended on their squatter community. They would come and gawk, big women and little children, old men who had little else to do each day but drink and sleep, and they would stand in the road like never-see-come-sees, and Jericha would come out of the house and into the road as if she were a tour guide, explaining each character to them proudly, showing off what her husband had done for her and her children. But her wayward daughters, knowing that this grand display made them the envy of the neighbourhood children (many of whom were poor and neglected and didn't always have enough to eat every day), would walk past the display holding their noses in the air, as if they had better things to do and more important people to meet. For Hamza and Jericha, however, this grandiose display brought out the child in each of them, and they relished the entire build-up of the season, as any happy child would have done, waiting for the climax of Christmas Day.

Jericha had a face like a knife that could cut you in two. Even though she had borne multiple children (the third and last for Hamza), in her midforties she still insisted on parading around the neighbourhood wearing skimpy, tight clothes to show off her curves and (she thought) incite lust in the hearts of any man she passed. But all the men of the village either were related to her in some way or thought of her pussy as old, tired, and probably AIDS-infested, stretched out from taking too much man prick over the years. After she would pass them, switching her sagging bottom in the road, they would sometimes comment quietly to each other about how Jericha had been bulling for KFC from time, jumping in the back of the maxi with the maxi man after school, sucking prick in the boys' toilet for small change, and climbing into cars with big hardback men when her pussy was only now starting to get pubes.

It was Jericha's mother, Jazmine, who had groomed her for this kind of life, who had let her know that her only asset was between her legs and that she needed to inveigle men as early as possible so that she could get as much out of them while she still had some firm flesh and elasticity left in her vagina. Jericha had set her eyes on Hamza when she was only fourteen, would watch him watching her from his gallery (waiting on his own daughters to return home from school). He, smoking a cigarette, would watch her climb backwards out of the taxi, showing off her rounded bottom in her short school skirt. She would then walk and roll, deliberately slowly, down the path, so that he could eat her with his eyes. Jericha marked that house, the nice two-storey yellow house with the red ixoras in the front yard, the Julie mango in the back, and a big moringa tree at the side. She saw Hamza's wife driving to and from work, a Dougla-looking woman with a heavy jaw, and she wondered where they got their money from. Was the wife the breadwinner, was it her family who had money and land, or was it his family, or ...? One day she saw Hamza escorting two uniformed policemen out the front door of the yellow house. The three men all paused on the patio. Jericha saw each of the policemen reach inside a planter and stick a package up under their bulletproof vest. She decided then and there that *she* was going to live in that yellow house one day.

But at the age of fourteen, even though she had set her eyes on Hamza, the fast life Jericha was living, and that she had been living since she had reached puberty, meant that she really didn't have too much time to study Hamza and his wife and three children in the yellow house. That was for down the road. Right now there was Jerry, the army man who had both a steady, decent income and a thing for young girls, and Everet, the middle-aged maxi man who let her ride to and from school each day for free, plus too bought her nice gifts like cellphones and jewellery and tennis shoes and sexy panties she would model for him after his shift was done. He would carry her into the cocoa and let her model those panties for him until he took them off with his teeth. The main thing that mattered to Jericha (besides the gifts they gave her) was that these men weren't one of her mother's seemingly constant stream of boyfriends who would invade their house fortnightly, cotching up on chairs or the couch, or leaving the bathroom door wide open, hoping she would sneak a peek at their wood while they were peeing. Men who adjusted their crotches when she passed, or tried to grab her hand when her mother wasn't looking and rest it on their prick, men who would swiftly and surreptitiously smack her on the bottom before she had time to jump out the way, men who found her cellphone number in her mother's phone and sent her dick pics late at night while her mother slept in the next room. By the time she was sixteen, she had graduated from Jerry and Everet to a gunman named Eyeball, and she felt badder than bad, especially when Eyeball told her that if any of her mother's boyfriends tried anything with her, he would fix to suit.

•

WHILE JERICHA WAS LIVING HER FAST LIFE, HAMZA KNEW IT was only a matter of time before Sweetie found out about the dark-ie making a baby for him in Tunapuna, or the three-year-old son he had up in Toco with another Nubian princess. She might even find out about the Jamaican bird at the Digicel outlet in City Gate that he was tracking — hard. Hamza had a weakness for dark chocolate. As much as he wanted to be faithful to Sweetie (who was more the colour of an unroasted coffee bean), his lustful eyes wandered and wandered and his dick wasn't ever far behind. Even that hot lil gyal from the squatter village, deep black like a too-lum — sometimes he would find his mind crossing on her when he was deep inside Sweetie, or when he was jocking he prick in the shower in the mornings. He'd heard that her name was Jericha and she was Jazmine's daughter from Crabhole Lane, and that she had some army man she was dealing with (or was it a maxi man?). He could wait. Time longer than rope.

The drugs game was good. Hamza had enough money to buy a few cars and put them on the road as taxis; he went into business with a bredren who wanted to start up a little mechanics shop in the village and who also had a link in the Bamboo to get chop-shop parts cheap; he invested in some weed whackers and rakes and chainsaws and started a yard-maintenance hustle; and he also financed a parlour for his sister-in-law to run, out of which he could also move some of his own merchandise. Sweetie got a new car leased every two years; she got her hair, eyebrows, and nails done weekly; she shopped for her clothes online; and he also got her a gym membership. Every Carnival he paid for her costume in Bliss, sometimes even a costume for her friend Leela, who had moved abroad and wanted to come home for Carnival and play mas. His child mothers (Toco and Tunapuna) got hair, nails, clothes, Pampers and milk, phone cards, toys, and jewellery for both his children and themselves. He was living large, people would say. He was a boss, a man amongst men, a real man, a village ram. But Hamza couldn't stop chasing. It was never enough — pussy, money, business. He could never just settle.

Jericha and Eyeball had been dealing for about eight months when she realized her period was late. She continued partying, drinking, smoking, wining, but when two months had passed and no blood had shown, she started to get worried. She asked her girlfriend Sheriqua what to do, and Sheriqua said, "Tell Eyeball."

Eyeball was suddenly scarce. When she called his phone, it rang out. She went looking for him in the little village off the Saddle Road that dwindled up into the San Juan hills. His place was locked up tight tight. After querying some of the neighbours, all she could learn was that he had gotten into a brown car with a set of men sometime Tuesday night. That had been two days ago. She walked back to the Saddle and caught a car back to her village, her hand resting on her increasingly hardening belly as the car swerved and rumbled on the beat-up road through the cocoa.

A few days later her girl Sheriqua came to tell her the news. "Jericha gyal, yuh hear about de man dat disappear? De one who now move back from foreign?"

"No."

"Well, is kidnap he was kidnap and de shout is is Eyeball and dem dat do eet!"

"*Nah,* gyal!"

"Oui! When last yuh talk to Eyeball?"

"Saturday past."

"Right. And up to now you cyan find he? *Cheups,* gyal, what you tink it is!"

Jericha didn't want to admit it, but she had heard Eyeball talk about kidnapping and how it was easy money. How there were rich men moving about Trinidad who were easy targets, men who were sorf sorf sorf and whose families could easily be pressed to cough up a good setta money. Indians mainly, but also some Syrians and French Creoles. A few times he had even pointed out some of these men to her. He had even gone so far as to tell her what nice things he would buy for her if he was to ever score that big a score.

A week after Jericha had gone looking for Eyeball, a week she had spent fretting and tossing and turning and wondering and worrying and feeling more and more nauseous, Eyeball suddenly showed up one night, tapping on her window so as not to wake her mother. Jericha opened the front door for him in her nightie. He tiptoed inside, and the two of them sat on the floor of her bedroom in the dark, leaning up against the bed.

"Where you was?" Jericha whispered.

"Gyallllll ..." He rubbed his head. She could barely make him out in the dark.

"Sheriqua and dem saying you was part of that kidnapping in Curepe — is true?" She hoped it wasn't. She didn't even know if she was going to tell him about the pregnancy. She had already been thinking about how to get rid of it.

Eyeball just kept sitting there with his head in his hands. He didn't know how to tell her. The plan had seemed so simple.

Tall-o had sworn de man had plenty plenty money, that in fact de man's whole family was rich, and dat it would be easy to get dem to give it up. So dey took de man from he driveway at gunpoint as he was gettin out of he van. Dey shove him in a nex car and drove far far far up into de bush, pass Arouca, somewhere by Aripo side. Dey get de man to call he family and tell dem is ransom dese men want — a million dollars. Whatever family answer de phone calmly responded that dis was impossible because de man dey had kidnap ent ha no million dollars jus res down someplace. De kidnappers hung up de phone.

It had never occurred to dem dat de plan would fail. Dey had to come up wit a nex plan.

Dey call de family back, dis time axing for half as much. De same family member relay de same information — dat was too much; dey was axing de impossible. Frustrated, dey hung up de phone a second time, and now dey force de man to walk, bound and gagged, tru de bush to a small encampment dey had set up. Dey beat him, frighten him, made him plead to de point where he pee heself. Den dey put him back on de phone. He beg his family to give dese men someting. "Is kill dey goin an kill me!" he said. De family said dey could get fifty tousand dollars togedda by de nex night. Would dey accept dat?

Tall-o respond, "We'll get back to you."

Dey were frustrated. Some men felt dat de family was lyin. Others were of de mind to take de money and run. Dey couldn't decide what to do. All dey knew was dat dey had been holdin dis man for eighteen hours and dey were hungry and tirsty. Eyeball and Batchac said they were goin down de road to de KFC to get supplies and would be back. Tall-o, Randy, and Jiggs were to stay wit de man.

Is when Eyeball and Batchac return to camp, dey realize it was all over. Jiggs, who had been tasked with watchmannin de fella, had chip off and beaten him so bad de man — who was frail to begin wit — had died. It seem Jiggs was upset dat he chile mudder was not answerin she phone, and dis had him tizik. Jiggs's story was dat de man say someting to him bout "Iz only a horn" and dat had set him off.

Now dey had to dispose of de body and cut their losses. Dey chop him up wit cutlasses and put de body parts in crocus bags, which dey trew down a ravine. Only de head dey bury. De man phone dey mash up wit a hammer and trew de bits and pieces out de window on dey drive back to San Juan.

All this replayed in Eyeball's mind as he leaned up against the bed in Jericha's room. But all he told her was "Gyal. Ah rell tyad." He stretched out on the floor right there and went to sleep.

•

HAMZA WAS IN THE LOCAL MERIKKKAN GOODZ OUTLET, A place he really enjoyed going to and which was totally worth the thirty U.S. dollar annual membership fee, as far as he was concerned. He always had to bring Jericha and her numerous family members here when he came, all squeezed up in the car, but once they reached the store, she and her people would go one way and he would go another. He enjoyed pushing his own cart up and down the aisles, marvelling at all the amazing things they had in foreign, that he could now buy here, things that screamed *foreign* in a way he had never experienced before in his little island country. He especially liked the way that Merikkkan Goodz celebrated the American holidays that no one in Trinidad did. When the U.S.

was having Black Friday for example, Merikkkan Goodz would advertise their own Black Friday deals, and it was guaranteed that Trinis would be lining up outside the doors of the store, early o'clock, and pushing and shoving to get in and fight each other down in the same manner they had seen Americans get on bad on social media. At Halloween time, the store would be festooned with fake jack-o'-lanterns and made-in-China witches and goblins and gossamer ghosts, fake autumn leaves hanging from the ceiling and the pillars; you could buy fake graves and fake vampires and fake cobwebs to decorate your house with, even though Halloween was not a Trinidadian tradition and had never been. At American Thanksgiving, too, seemingly hundreds of imported, hormonally engorged monster turkeys filled freezer after freezer, alongside exquisite maple-flavoured and wood-smoked hams from Iowa and North Carolina farms. Hamza had no idea where these places were or what they looked like, but it made him want to go there and see for himself.

This particular day that Hamza was in Merikkkan Goodz, it happened to be Thanksgiving season. He was perusing the aisles and employees were already busy stocking shelves for Christmas. He saw an employee stocking a shelf full of small nativity scenes, ones that lit up when you plugged them in, the kind that was a household fixture back in the day, resting on the TV/stereo combination console that people used to have in their living rooms, taking pride of place. Hamza recognized that light-up nativity scene from his childhood, and suddenly he was flooded with memories of that home at Christmastime, his mother and grandmother baking black cakes, filling the house with a heavenly, rich scent, while his father would be out hunting for wild meat to curry. The year Hamza turned ten, his father brought him along on the hunt, the first time he had ever done so. Throughout the boy's childhood, Hamza's father had rarely engaged with him, almost never touched him, and had left the child rearing up to Hamza's mother and his aunts and grandmothers. But on this day, Hamza's father not only paid attention to him, he spoke to him, and looked him straight in the eye. They were hunting for manicou and maybe some tattoo if they could find one deep in the bush. The skeletal hunting dogs, deliberately starved to make them "better hunters," flushed out all manner of prey: iguanas, agouti, and finally a young manicou, which Hamza successfully killed with a small air rifle. For the first time in Hamza's life, his father smiled at him.

The nativity scene jolted Hamza back to this happier time and put him in a mood to celebrate a *real* Christmas. He started piling up the cart with every Christmas decoration he could find, and it was on this day that he decided to populate the yard of his house with multiple inflatable decorations. He had to drop Jericha and her family back home, grab his van, return to the store, and load the tray of the van with boxes containing at least ten giant inflatable Christmas characters; the pump to blow them up; yards and yards of Christmas lights; two rotating laser light globes; red mesh stockings to be hung up around the house; wreaths of every description; tinsel in green, red, and gold; and three fake Christmas trees in different sizes.

It became a divine obsession. Hamza set up the inflatable characters around the yard, arranging and rearranging them, trying to work out the perfect composition. Sometimes he would ask for Jericha's input, but Jericha, feeling dumb, would only agree to whatever Hamza decided. The first year of the set-up, to accompany the whole display he streamed a foreign radio station that played old-time Christmas music performed largely by White artists — Bing Crosby, Dean Martin, Frank Sinatra — and blasted these songs from his inside stereo. This baffled the neighbours, who were accustomed to hearing Caribbean Christmas music, such as parang or soca parang, or compilations of reggae-ized Christmas songs. Instead, Hamza was enamoured of one-horse open sleighs and white snow and jingle bells and frosty snowmen.

The arranging of the massive figures became an annual ritual. The second year of the inflatable characters, Hamza decided he needed to cast the dirt yard first. He dug up all the flowers and bushes and vegetables and the patch of corn and everything he had been growing and tending to for the past year, and one Saturday he got Jericha to recruit the pumpkin-vine men of her family to ceremoniously cast the whole of the front yard in concrete. This allowed Hamza a proper stage on which to better secure and arrange the inflatable characters and allowed people, especially little children, to walk amongst them. When the multitude of string lights were set up around the yard and the house and the inflatable characters waved in the December evening breeze, it became, for both Hamza and Jericha, their own magical winter wonderland. The only thing missing was snow. Hamza began researching how he could acquire some fake snow — that would be for the following year. What Hamza did invest in was a fifteen-hundred-watt speaker system to blast his own curated mix of Christmas carols throughout the neighbourhood. This included a medley of cheesy Christmas carols sung by an obscure Scandinavian band, their ABBA-ish accents wafting across the valley:

He come from the glory.
He come from the glorious kingdom!
He come from the glory.
He come from the glorious kingdom!
Oh yes!

Hamza would put the ten songs of this specific collection on repeat and play it endlessly, obsessed with his annual Christmas tasks of cleaning, painting, and decorating. Morning, noon, and night the neighbours were subjected to the equivalent of brainwashing or Chinese water torture. The sound waves from the speaker system so intense they shook the glass in their windows, and the inane lyrics left an indelible print in the involuntary listeners' minds, haunting them like the aural equivalent of persistence of vision whenever Hamza decided to give his music a rest. The cover of the old Jim Reeves tune "Señor Santa Claus" was a particular favourite of Hamza's, and he would beat it to death like a road march.

Jericha once again took up her post as tour guide, showing the Christmas wonderland to the villagers and yet even more pumpkin-vine family who had driven from other villages farther afield to come and gawk. As usual, her stush daughters had no time for what, to them, was now an even bigger pappyshow than the previous year, and the corny music that Hamza blasted like a daily mantra made the whole garish display even more of an embarrassment. They walked past the display each day as if it weren't there, and went and hung out at their cousins' and aunts' and other assorted relatives' houses in the squatter community.

Hamza noted their attitude and it pained him. He regretted not having created such a spectacle with his first family, and sometimes in the evenings, he would sit outside by himself, smoking a cigarette, watching the inflatable characters sway in the breeze, and imagine what his first family would have done if he had provided this for them. He reminisced about the Christmas after his first son was born. He and Sweetie has been so young and so in love. He had been quite dashing back then, with his piercing black eyes, heavy brows, and wavy jet-black hair. And Sweetie had been stunning, with her Coca-Cola–bottle shape, her streaked brown-blond hair piled high on her head (all natural, no weave), and those sugary lips he had loved to kiss. Their son was a wonder to them, and resembled Hamza definitively, so he knew no one could say he get jacket. Just prior to that Christmas he had carried a few kilos of coke from Cedros into Port-of-Spain and had been paid handsomely for it, so he took that money, and he and Sweetie went to Maraj Jewellers and bought plenty gold jewellery for the boy — some items (like a tiny baby bangle) that the baby could wear now, and others (rope chains and rings and bands) to be put away for when he got older. Hamza bought a real toy car for his son, big enough that he could ride in it, and a giant stuffed giraffe, and for Sweetie he bought a matching diamond earring and necklace set.

Hamza would fondly remember these days in the evenings as he sat outside alone, Jericha having wandered off, as was her habit, to circulate amongst her pumpkin-vine family in the squatter community adjacent to their house. She could only sit for so long in the yard and watch him work; then it was as if her foot got hot, and off she would go. This bothered Hamza, though he never said anything. He never followed her into that realm, the squatter community, but would wait patiently for her to return, never asking where she had been or whom she had seen.

•

JERICHA HAD THE BABY AFTER ALL, A BABY GIRL. SHANIQUA tried to throw her a small baby shower, but she was miserable and blue, what with Eyeball in jail and no money coming in, stuck at her mother's house, and her mother now vex that she would "have a gran to mine." Once Jericha's belly had reached a certain size, she had to stop partying and drinking and dressing up in revealing outfits, because people just watched her sideways as if she wasn't all there. Sometimes she really felt she wasn't all there in truth. Eyeball and the others had gone to jail for murder once police had dug up the head of the man and eventually (directed by Jiggs) recovered the two crocus bags as well. Jericha knew she was truly on her own, what with this black baby, no child father, no money, and no prospects.

Sheriqua had brought the baby a blond doll as a gift. Jericha held it in her hand for a second, studying it, touching the hair, before carefully placing it in the child's crib. She was remembering another blond doll, a blond Barbie, that an aunt had sent her in a barrel from foreign. She had been so proud of this doll and had carried it everywhere with her. The other kids, jealous of this fancy foreign gift, stole the doll from her one day, cut off all its hair, and then took a black felt marker and tried to colour all the pale pinky-beige skin in black ink. They then returned it to Jericha, letting her know that now it "look like she." Jericha had hidden the doll for a few days after that, feeling ashamed, and eventually concealed it in a cereal box, a makeshift coffin, and threw both in the trash heap at the back of the village.

Eyeball was going to be in jail for a long time. It was now November, and in Trinidad the circuit of parties was starting up that would run through Christmastime, into the new year, and straight through Carnival. A good four to five months of fêting, wining, and trying to squeeze as much money out of every man-jack she encountered for the season. She asked Sheriqua to fix her up with a new weave; she got her cousin to front her a set of acrylic nails; she begged and borrowed clothes and shoes from her girl-friends and family members. All she needed was to hook some man to carry her out. The baby — named Didi — was sometimes left with her mom (for a fee), sometimes left with her younger sister, and sometimes with her sister's boyfriend. It didn't take long for Jericha to be back in action: she went to a birthday party for a second cousin of hers down the road from her village, and after wining, splitting, back backing, and throwing her leg in the air a few times, she had men tracking her for her phone number. This time of year men were lavish with their spending. They wanted a hot gyal to ramp with, and Jericha soon began to acquire the new clothes, shoes, wigs, nails, eyelashes, and hair that doubled her appeal. In a few weeks, she had graduated to dudes paying for her groceries, Pampers and milk for Didi, and drivers. One fella brought her a new cellphone, while a next one brought her jewel-lery she could floss with.

By Easter the circuit was done, and Jericha had not put a single dime aside for the guava season. But she had shared much of her earnings with her mother while the getting was good, and so she knew she could cruise through for a while on her mother's meagre income until another opportunity arose. The problem now was that she was throwing up again in the morning, her clothes were feeling tight, and her breasts were suddenly bulging out of her bra. She had used condoms right through the party season (as far as she could remember), but there was that one time a condom had slipped off and ... She knew she didn't want this baby, not with Didi barely a year old and Eyeball still lock up. She just didn't know what to do. An abortion was out of the question; it was illegal, to begin with, and there was no child father she could trap into paying an exorbitant sum at the private clinics. She was not going to take her chances with the backyard abortionists, as she knew of girls who had been severely damaged or even died trying that route. Jericha drank warm Guinness; she overdosed on senna tea and worming pills, hoping these would have some effect, but all they did was empty her guts for a week, and she felt even more nauseous than before. In desperation, she decided to look up Everet, the maxi man that she had dealt with as a school girl. She still saw him driving maxi in her village, still hailed him every time she saw him, and had even ridden in his maxi from time to time when she was unable to find a driver. He always took the opportunity to fondle her knee when she sat up next to him, and if his other passengers were out of earshot, would reminisce on their spicy times back in the cocoa. Last she heard, he had married a Spanish Baptist woman from La Pastora, but that did not deter Jericha from putting her plan into play.

One rainy Thursday afternoon, Jericha put on a clingy, almost see-through dress that barely covered her crotch, and, cradling an oversized umbrella, went looking for Everet's maxi in the village. When he beeped her and pulled up to the curb, she quickly slid into the familiar passenger seat up front, flashing him a big smile.

"I was looking for you!" she breathed at him.

He immediately started flirting with her. By the time they reached San Juan, she had told him a story about her boyfriend who beat her, and she let him know that she missed having a "real man" in her life, one who knew how to treat a lady. When he asked her if she was getting out at the Croisee in San Juan, she asked if she could ride with him on his route as she needed "a friend" she could talk to. They continued to chat all the way back up Saddle Road while Everet worked his maxi, and when he let off the last passenger in Pipiol Road, he turned the maxi around, and they headed back down the Saddle to Mount Hololo, and their usual turnoff into the cocoa. Jericha knew she couldn't get pregnant twice, so she rode the old red man until he was sweating and flustered and out of breath. He never offered to put on a condom and she never asked for one, and so she knew everything would work out just as she had planned.

When she braced Everet a month later and let him know she was making a child for him and he would have to take care of her and the baby or she would tell his new wife, Everet wasn't really bothered. In his youth he had made a few children here and there with various women and had always done his part by ensuring his children had food and clothes and school fees. He actually felt excited that he would be having another child so late in life. He told Jericha, "Dohn worry — ah go see yuh get yuh money," closed the door of the maxi, and drove off.

•

HAMZA HAD ALWAYS KEPT HIS EYE ON JERICHA, EVER SINCE those days when he had watched her back backing out of the taxi in her school uniform, cocking her bamsie in the air, sometimes flashing him the pink or white panties she had on under her plaid skirt. He would feel his dick get hard in his drawers and sometimes would have to go back in the house before anyone saw, Sweetie or his kids. Hamza saw when Jericha got her first belly, and heard the shout that it was Eyeball's, and then heard that Eyeball was doing time for murder. It was then that he felt somewhat sorry for her, and this new concern lessened some of his lustfulness. But when the child was born and he saw her carrying the pretty black baby around on her hip, and then afterward, when he saw her figure return, his lustfulness returned with it. Not long after, he heard she had made a next child, another girl, only this time the paternity was in question. The second child was fair-skinned, nothing like her mother or Eyeball. It was anybody's guess. Hamza was no fool, and he knew what kind of life Jericha had been living, but for some reason he also had a soft spot for her even though they had never actually spoken. Once, at Carnival, he went to watch mas in the village and take a drink with his friend who ran the mechanics shop he had helped finance. He saw her there, wining low in the main road in a raffia skirt costume and a beaded bra top, a rainbow lei around her neck. The band's theme was "Sailors Ashore," and when a particularly popular song came on, he saw her backside tremble and he heard men lining the sidewalk shout out in appreciation, and as she bent over and trembled it even harder, she looked directly at Hamza and winked. Hamza was transfixed. Despite everything, there was something about this girl/woman that drove him mad. He grinned back at her, his dick hard like a rock. The time now seemed shorter than the rope.

Jazmine, Jericha's mother, had been secretly orchestrating a union between her daughter and Hamza for years. Like her daughter, Jazmine had always admired the yellow house with the ixoras and the upstairs gallery; she knew Hamza was a man of means, someone who had not only made money but had invested it, and Jazmine had been steadily conniving how to get her daughter into that house and displace Hamza's wife and children. Jazmine especially coveted the small servant's quarters at the back of the house and knew that it would be a perfect mother-in-law apartment for her in her old age. Now that Jericha had two children by two different men, and only one known child father (who was in jail and not coming out anytime soon), she felt there was no more time to delay.

"Jericha," she said one day, as her daughter was breastfeeding Kiki while Didi played on the floor. "You not getting any younger and neither am I. I don't want to be living in this rundown shack when I get too old to move around too good, yuh hear me?"

"Yes, Ma."

"So hear what — yuh see that Indian man in the yellow house? Hamza?"

"Yeah?"

"You know that man real dotish fuh yuh. You know ah bet dat man go leave he wife fuh yuh if yuh play yuh cards right!"

"Eh-heh?"

"What do you say? I can arrange everything. I know exactly who to go to."

Jericha knew her mother meant the old obeah man in Carenage. She had taken Jericha there a few times as a child, and she knew her mother still went there on the regular to deal with all manner of things.

"Ma. I been watching that house for years, yuh know. It too sweet. But how you go get rid of the wife? An his chirren?"

"Dohn worry. Just leave that up to me. You just need to make sure you making a child for he before the end of this year and she will clear out, truss meh."

•

IT WAS NOW CHRISTMAS DAY AND HAMZA MADE SURE TO start blasting the music from all 7:30 a.m. He had to wash the driveway with Breeze for the umpteenth time, just to make sure every tile was spotless. Jericha did her usual disappearing act short-ly after breakfast, and so Hamza was left on his own to handle everything. He puffed away on a Du Maurier and opened his first beer of the day, to be chased later on with puncheon and sorrel. He could see the neighbours in their yard, making screw faces. They had already called the police on him for the loud music, but he knew they would never dare to pull that on Christmas Day. He inspected the glittering, swaying, inflatable characters, glistening and gleaming in the Caribbean sunshine, knowing that they would hold court for only a few more weeks, and then they would be packed back in their storage boxes to await another year. He didn't know exactly what he would do with the yard after they were put away. He didn't know if it made sense to plant anything or set up a small parlour on the newly cast ground, an idea he had been musing about, maybe something to keep Jericha busy and keep her black ass home. He couldn't help but think of Sweetie and how hard she had worked, even though he could have easily provided for both of them. His former wife was an industrious and level-headed woman who had taken pride in helping out her hus-band. He puffed harder on the Du Maurier, trying not to recollect the Christmas Eve phone call from his Toco child mother, telling him how she was dying of AIDS. He didn't want to think if he would be here next year to set up the inflatable characters, to adorn the Christmas house. He had also heard that Eyeball was out of jail, had even heard he had come by the house looking for Jericha and the daughter he had never seen.

Hamza spent most of Christmas Day alone in the yard in his winter wonderland, wandering amongst the inflatable characters and in and out of the house, cranking the music louder and louder, trying to drown out the encroaching thoughts in his head. A few times during the day, Jericha, followed by her conceited daughters, sauntered into the yard, causing him to momentarily perk up, but then they would saunter back out again, to go traipsing around the squatter village, supposedly visiting her pumpkin-vine family. He wondered if she was fucking Eyeball already, and if not, how long before she would. He had a sharpened cutlass ready if it came to that. He hated her. He hated her and he didn't know why he loved her, too, and couldn't seem to just put her in her place.

The neighbours were glaring at him again from their gallery. He cranked the music even louder: "*Faaaall on your kneeees! Oh heeeear the angels voiiiiices.*" He stared blankly back at them. It was a couple who lived across the street. The woman never left the yard except in her husband's company. He hated them as well. He hated everyone, even himself. He went in the house and poured a glass of puncheon and forgot the sorrel. It was getting dark now. The Christmas house blinked and shone and danced and swayed and Hamza knew this was it — this was his life's work. His own children hated him, his stepchildren hated him, Sweetie hated him, and Jericha despised him as well. He wondered what they would put on his tombstone. He wondered if Jericha would even put a tombstone on his grave at all. He wondered if Eyeball would be setting up the Christmas characters next year, living in his house with Jericha at his side, showing off to everyone in the village.

Miguel Street Redux

The first time I heard her, I rushed outside the house, alarmed, fearing someone was being murdered.

"Ooooooooooo Gaaaaawwwd, oooo Jeeeeeeesuuuus Laaaaaawwwwd. I thank you, Jesus, for allll aiiyyyeeeeeeeeeee, oh Gawd, o Laaaawd, Heavenly Faaaaahder!"

Where was this godawful sound coming from? It was up; I looked up into the night sky, then to my right — apparently the apartment building next door.

"That's how she is. Every night," NP stated in his usual unassuming way. As if it was all so normal now.

"Oooooo Gaaaaawd, ooo Laaaawd, Laaaaaaaaaaaaaaaaaawd." She sobbed between screams: *Uhunh! Unhunh!* "Help me, Jeeeesuuuuus. Oooooh Gaaaawd, I thank you, Faaahderrrrr. Ooo gaaaaaawd!" *Uunnnhhhhhh hunh hunh!*

"The first time I heard it, I thought someone was being murdered too." He then went back to his cigarette and his video game. Shrieking at the top uh she lungs. Bawling out she soul case. As if she being murdered in truth.

I didn't know quite what to make of this. I had never heard anyone having a religious experience where they sounded as if they were in utter and devastating — even fatal — pain. It was excruciating to listen to. I had seen people possessed by spirit before, rolling all on the ground in Orisha and Spiritual Baptist feast, but this was some nother level shit. It did not sound nice.

We had just moved into the neighbourhood — working class for sure, but *decent*, churchgoing working class — and although it wasn't the nicest house or nicest area, we had to take what we could get, both for financial reasons and because we needed our dogs with us and not every landlord was agreeable to pets. It had never occurred to me that the property would come with its own unhinged soundtrack.

A few nights later I went to pee in the back bathroom, and in the dead of night I could hear the faint drone of what sounded like Islamic music coming from the same apartment building next door. Hypnotic and melodic. I thought I knew this song from another time: it sounded like "Salil Sawarim," the ISIS soundtrack in the glossy viral video starring the Trini bredda who had gone across to Syria to fight holy war. He was now on the cover of all the newspapers, his family being interviewed on the seven o'clock news. I tried not to read too deeply into all this and went back to bed. In the morning, up to pee again, I was amazed to hear the same music droning from the neighbour's window. *What the hell was going on over there?* One screaming and bawling for Jesus, another planning jihad. What de actual fuck. Okay, I really didn't know if this was ISIS music, but it was Islamic music I was hearing, and coming from the little hole in the wall that it was, I had my suspicions. *National Geographic,* CNN, *and* Al Jazeera had labelled Trinidad the new hotbed of terrorism cells in the Western hemisphere. Anything was possible.

By Ole Year's Night we had a new madness to add to the mix. A drunken middle-aged lady had just moved in on the other side of the same apartment building and, deciding to throw a party to christen the place, was keeping us up all night and into the morning with she tabanca songs, having a full-on rockers reggae session. An old CD was left on repeat and at maximum volume (while she left the premises? Whole day? Or pass out from too much puncheon?), and we had to hear Pinchers, Freddie McGregor, Beres Hammond, *and* Gregory Isaacs on and on, ad infinitum for at least sixteen hours, until I asked NP if he coulda throw a scratch bomb through she window, please, and end the torment.

This apartment building became the soundtrack to our lives. Jesus Bawling Soul Case Lady screaming so much we once had to go by the police station (no lie) and file a report. Rockers Lady still throwing she weekend parties (she even strung out a line of coloured lights and put some metal chairs and a fake palm tree, trying to make her patio a small bar; we began to wonder if she was making fares in there and hence the reason why the music playing so loud). At certain intervals we would — in addition — hear a conch shell blowing from across the street, when the pundit came to visit the Hindu family in the nice ample upstairs house, neighbours we barely saw, who lived behind big, electronic gates. And every year on my birthday, the Church of St. John the Baptist, situated up the side street from us, would come dancing and stepping out with their red-and-white robes (*Kawooooo* Kabiosile!), heads tied, staffs in hand, drumming, chanting, stepping, breathing, *ah-hunh ah-hunh!*, come down de lane, right in front we wall, to turn around again and go back up de lane, chanting, heaving, drumming, and I would raise the little black puppy above the wall to watch the goings-on. The puppy would be silent, transfixed, to see these people with drum and flambeau making space at the road juncture.

From Friday nights until Sunday afternoons it was the multitude of house-front and real brick-and-mortar Pentecostal, fundamentalist, full gospel, Church of God, and Nazarene places of worship raising a holy cacophony in de place. Competing choirs — some filled with ruction and spirit, some stunningly off-key — would clash across our backyard, the churches themselves situated on parallel streets. Unlike the Church of St. John the Baptist, the songs they sang were decidedly un-Caribbean to my ear. There was no syncopation; there was no clave, no African drumming, no call-and-response. These were European melodies, European rhythms, which distressed me no end. Even more distressing were the few times I glimpsed a White, male, Southern-accented preacher — respected guest and invitee of these American-based churches — holding court and brainwashing the Black masses who sat humbly and often dejectedly in the makeshift pews in front of him. These were poor-people churches, the only exception being the big, fancy, two-storey Nazarene church to the west of us; that congregation was a fashion show every Sunday, five-inch red bottoms, BMWs, and Lexuses.

Monday to Friday there were the endless cars, their sound systems blasting and blaring and shaking windows with the most explicit and unnecessary over-the-top lyrics to make you freeze in midaction in your house where you are minding yuh own damn business. Like the day I hear a sweet voice sing out a most explicit description of vaginal penetration including the textbook-correct names of body parts, at *full* volume, inna dancehall riddim, on a Wednesday, at high noon. I had to stop what I was doing. Not … even … an … *attempt* at disguise, no double entendre, no metaphor, no *cyat, pussy, toonee, banana, cassava, cane* — nuttin but raw clinical and brazen lyrics. Aural rape in my own home.

The daily and nightly auditory assault on my being was only bolstered by the never-ending dust that seemed to seep into every crack and crevice in our house. (Truth be told, some of the glass louvres were missing in the drawing room, so that didn't help.) I couldn't understand how I could clean and clean and clean and still this fine layer of dust just kept appearing and appearing. I eventually learned that this dust came with the Sahara dust storms, huge clouds of powdered sand that made the journey from the Sahara Desert in North Africa, across the Middle Passage, to finally collapse in the Caribbean. The same journey that millions of enslaved Africans took to reach this tiny island, these same minuscule particles of earth now took, relentlessly, insistently. I found myself wondering exactly how much of Africa was being transported and deposited in the Caribbean. Was this like a horizontal hourglass, one in which, eventually, over thousands and thousands of years, Africa would end up in the Caribbean? Could this be a way the Caribbean was compensating for coastal erosion and rising sea levels due to climate change? I was sure that the dust carried stories. It wanted to reunite with long-lost kin. Jumbies that could not return to Guinea beckoned Guinea to come to them.

Along the same street with the madhouse apartment building, the endless stream of cars day and night, and the never-ending dust seeping in, were the regulars. Marathon Man could be seen, equally day and night, walking the street til his shoes buss out. He would change to slippers and persist on his continual jaunts, seemingly non-stop, couldn't sit still, always on a mission. What motivated him? Was it spirit lash have him so, I wondered. Uncle (he was an elderly man, wearing wire-rimmed spectacles, with a full white beard and the remaining hair on his balding head white also) pounding that pavement morning, noon, and evening, until his calves knotted in hard bulges and you could see the cut grooves in his thighs, although he must have been in his sixties. Pradesh, the fella who did bring de gas, used to complain that no matter how much gym he went to, he could "never look as buff as dese crackheads." "Fadda like you routin, yuh routin!" he used to tease, but Marathon Man was too busy to respond. On a mission. NP said it was only a mission to find rocks, but I wasn't convinced that was all it was.

There was a next one, Teddy, who was much more sinister. I didn't like him at all. As I saw him passing, I would move quick quick into the house. All because, when we first moved into the neighbourhood, I was in the yard minding the dogs when I looked up to see this man standing like a stone in the road, staring at me. Through me. Right through me. Not a waver, a flicker. Didn't say nothing. Just stared and stared in a way that made me want to go inside the house. So I did, and told NP about it. He told me every man did stare at me, with my big bottom, but that was just him. I couldn't shake the feeling that something was wrong with Teddy. His eyes — they were blank. There was nothing behind them.

Then came the night of the snake. A big macajuel appeared in the yard and NP needed to get it out because of the dogs, but the neighbour (not the Jesus Bawling Soul Case Lady or ISIS Recruit or Rockers Lady, but a next neighbour quite at the end of the garden, a Rasta at that), wanted to kill it. Anything — iguana, snake, manicou — to him, everything had to dead. This neighbour was supposedly a big drugs man (NP had heard talk), but there you have it — a supposed Rasta who was also a drugs man preaching the murderation of Jah's creatures. Then and there I baptized him Natty Dead. NP went in the house to look for the phone number for the wildlife rescue people, but while he was gone Snakey decide to buss it and made the fatal mistake of climbing Natty Dead wall. Next we heard one set of screaming and bawling from the whole crew of Natty's children (Natty had followed the words of Jah that said, "Go forth and multiply"). Then nothing, silence. NP looked like he was about to cry. I secretly hoped that Snakey had somehow managed to manoeuvre and weave her way through the giant chenette tree and maybe make it to another tree and another and stay in that canopy, evading the hatred and stupidity of humans. But I wasn't entirely optimistic.

This same Rastaman had a cock that crowed the first five notes to Herb Alpert and the Tijuana Brass's "The Lonely Bull" every morning — over and over, ad infinitum. I began to take it as a sign. The place was beginning to speak to me, but in ways that made me uneasy. Within a two- or three-block radius, we had the Jesus Bawling Soul Case Lady and the ISIS Recruit and the Hindus and the Spiritual Baptists and the Pentecostals and the Rastas. Yet, in all this beautiful diversity, this multicultural all-o'-we-is-one patriotic wet dream, there was some kind of stench that kept permeating the air — literally. The septic tank for the apartment building full of characters out of a Naipaul novel was overflowing, and some nights we had to close up all the windows just to be able to breathe, and to keep out the increasingly visible cockroaches that were thriving in that cesspit.

I had a habit of sitting on the gallery every evening with my laptop (neighbours and macocious passersby like Teddy and Marathon Man be damned), to escape NP's cigarette smoke and the drone of the TV. I was either working online or, in between work, writing stories I hoped to publish one day. One particular evening as I was sitting there, I heard *ratatatatatataataatat!* coming from the hillsides. I froze.

"Did you hear that?"

"What?"

"That sound. Sounded like gunfire."

NP was busy trying to kill some soldiers in the video game he was playing. A cigarette was dangling from his lip, smoke curling up and causing him to squint. He wasn't taking me on.

Brrrrrrrtttttttttt!

I jumped up. Nervously called the dogs in from the yard.

"Whaddya doin? Gyal, dat gunfire so far away! *Cheeupsssss.*"

I couldn't relax. How did he know how far away it was? Bullets could travel far, oui!

"But that is gunfire!"

"*So?*" He paused the game to watch me straight in my face. "What that hadta do wit *we*? Boy, I grew up with gunfire around me my whole life, *right* outside my door, bodies in the street ..." NP began to rattle off reminiscences of his childhood war days in Laventille.

I didn't really want to hear this right then. I wanted to be somewhere *safe*. The shitty old glass louvres that were the frontage of the house, some broken, others missing, did not foster confidence in me that I would be protected from a stray bullet. The dogs, as unconcerned as NP with this new development, were busy sniffing around for lizards.

I became more strident. "*Dogs! Inside! Now!*"

"Why you getting on so?" NP was now annoyed.

"Because is *guns!*"

BOOM!

That one rattled the house, the walls, the shitty louvres. The dogs, suddenly subdued, filed into the house obediently.

NP paused his game again. "Okay, that sounded close."

"Yuh *see?*" I was almost pleading.

"Yeah."

He turned off the lights. Began to peer through the louvres like that picture of Malcolm X with the rifle. *By any means necessary.* The dogs lay down.

This kind of scenario became more and more frequent. Every few nights it would be the same thing. The occasional *Pow! Boom!* coming from the hillsides that bordered our neighbourhood (not right at our doorstep, but not too far away neither), generally followed by a *ratatatat* or *brrrrtttt*, letting us know which new machinery dem yutes up dey had recently acquired. Sometimes, just to keep us on our toes, a *pow!* or *boom!* would come from a different direction, sometimes sounding real close, and that just added more tension and anxiety to the thickening milieu.

Then came the day when they found the man body hanging half-in, half-out de car. Blood everywhere, someone had gunned him down while he was driving, the car stopped at a crazy angle, and he had attempted to exit before fully expiring right dey. Right dey dead. Just a few blocks from us. We weren't home at the time, but when I passed by the spot a few days later, I could still see the darkened bloodstains on the pavement.

I had done my research on the area before we moved in. Google searches for *crime* and *shootings* and *killings* and *murder* cross-checked with the names of the town and the streets nearby. I knew this level of bloodshed I was seeing was not normal. It was unprecedented. But this was also happening across the island now. There were no more hot spots. Everywhere was a hot spot.

Soon thereafter I involuntarily surrendered my freedom. I used to war with NP on an almost daily basis about being able to go to the store on my own while he was at work. The store was only three blocks away, on the main road. I'm a big woman, I would say to him, I accustom to doing my own thing and getting my own thing and not relying on nobody for nuttin. He would argue that it was "nuttin" for me to wait until he got home and we could go together. If I wanted us to walk, we could walk, or we could take the car, but just don't go out alone. In the last neighbourhood we had lived in, it had been easy — crime was infrequent and there were plenty of businesses on the route to and from the grocery, lots of traffic, pedestrians, even a police station I would have to pass. But here, in this place, all I would pass were rows of shut-up houses, or houses converted into churches, or abandoned properties overgrown with vines and weeds; questionable cars with questionable occupants, tinted down windows, shady yutemen eyein me up. It used to vex me no end, how people like Marathon Man and the menacing Teddy could route the road whole day and night and never have to worry or think twice about their safety (well, I guess crack addiction could do that to you). The point was, I was now prisoner in my home, behind gates and louvres, no car and no licence neither, beholden to a husband and a fear for my own safety.

Incidences (which is an understatement) began to escalate. There was a sudden rash of taxi-driver murders — so even if I had anticipated jumping in a taxi, who knows if I could have ended up in a similar situation? The modus operandi was always the same: taxi man would pick up a passenger, and while driving would end up with either an ice pick in the back of the neck or a slashed throat. And yet life went on. I saw people still travelling in taxis — what choice did they have? It was like things were happening but not happening, and the apathy and numbness made everything seen more unsettling.

I continued to read the newspapers assiduously, and watched the evening news too. The characters in my neighbourhood suddenly became more sinister — or tragic. What had really happened to Jesus Bawling Soul Case Lady to make her scream so? I began to wonder if she had seen her family members murdered before her eyes at some point. And what about ISIS Recruit? Was he/she/they really planning an Islamic coup in the country, as had already been attempted in 1990? Was I living next to a stockpile of arms, grenades, bombs? Was Rockers Lady making fares in her home because her husband had been slaughtered, beheaded, dumped in the sea to resurface days later, bloated and bleached white? Or had she had to flee a relationship because her "close family relative" had threatened to kill her, chop her up, and put her body parts in a barrel? The newspaper stories I read on a daily basis began to meld and dissolve into my everyday world. What started off as a cast of jokey characters from an old-time Naipaul novel was now turning into a grisly horror story. Maybe Natty Dead was the kingpin for a gang that traded in machines, Venezuelans, and cocaine. Gang war could pop off at any time if that were the case, and we would be right in the middle of it. This was not the old Trinidad of my father's day, the happy-go-lucky, multiracial, all-o'-we-is-one world of Woodbrook circa the 1940s, with Wrigley-chewing American soldiers as backdrop. There was something diabolical going on here.

One of our beloved dogs, Ebony, defending her yard, bit a crapaud one night and succumbed quickly to the toad's poison. She was dead within minutes. Even though NP had thoroughly screened and meshed down the yard, even though we had been certain to seal any holes in the red-brick perimeter walls, somehow crapaud still managed to invade. And not no small crapaud neither — big, stinking, fat, squat crapaud. Crapaud fadda. It was one of these Ebony bit, and then she died. We buried her in the backyard, and that's when I began to notice something even more strange.

When NP began digging the grave, he hit upon a cement box partially submerged in the earth. The lid of this box had partially disintegrated, but I could make out what looked like implements inside — a shepherd's crook, several machetes, chains. When NP saw this he actually turned pale (no small feat for him), and I knew we had disturbed something we were not supposed to mess with. He stopped digging in that part of the yard and resumed digging Ebony's grave far away.

Later I asked him about it. "What do you think that box was about?"

"I dunno. Some Shango thing. I ent messin with it."

I wanted to know more, but knew I would have to be skillful in getting NP onside. He didn't like any "obeah ting."

"Okay, well, I'm thinking we should probably find out in case we need to move."

He was quiet then. We both knew what I meant.

"I'll ask around," he finally said. "Some of the elders in the neighbourhood. Maybe they can tell us something."

NP went and talked to Mother, the old old woman who had been running a parlour out of her yard for donkey years, the kind of parlour lady who might dig in her cleavage and give you some change out of her left breast.

He came back with the report: "This was a yard. An Orisha yard. They used to hold big feast and all kinda ting. Mother said from way back when she was a little girl, and people would come from far, from South and ting. She said Teddy and Marathon Man used to be up in it too."

"What!"

"Yep. An den something happened. And the ole lady who ran the yard did somebody something and it came back on her, and Mother says they found her in the yard. Like, corbeaux led them to she."

I was speechless. This was not good at all.

"Well, that explains the box, then."

"Yep."

I knew Yorubans had come from Africa to this country as free people — not as slaves — and had kept their religion and their rituals. One of the only places in the Caribbean this had happened. Maybe this whole area had once been a free Yoruban village. It made sense — this *was* a power spot, and that's why so many different creeds and spirits were drawn to the neighbourhood: Spiritual Baptist, fundamentalist Christian, Hindu, Muslim, Rastafarian. Perhaps even before this Orisha yard there had been a temple here, before Yorubans, before Europeans, a sacred spot of the Nepoya, Kalina, Warao, or Kalipuna.

The problem was, it was an *abandoned* power spot. Whatever had occurred here had broken the power, perverted it. Those energies that had once been adored were now neglected. Neglected and forgotten. And scorned too.

NP said quietly, "You know these African spirits not resting easy with all these born-agains hanging around."

He was right. How many of these Christian holier-than-thou flocks were busy mocking and denigrating African spirits every Sunday, even though they themselves were the descendants of these same Africans? The Catholic priest in the cavernous cathedral on the main road was even worse, talking about devil worship and primitive heathenism. Maybe these abandoned spirits were riding the people who lived here, the occupants of the Miguel Street redux apartment block next door to us, Teddy and Marathon Man, Natty Dead ...

I now saw that this sense of abandonment and neglect permeated the whole neighbourhood. Too many boarded-up houses, half-burnt dwellings that had been left to rot and be reclaimed by bush, concrete foundations that were left to disintegrate, crazy staircases going nowhere hanging off half-built houses. Several of these premises had been left behind by families who had migrated. The older, completed houses stayed locked up, seemingly uninhabitable, until some family member abroad croaked and then the land would be sold off to a developer, who would build six- and eight-unit apartment blocks on the lots like the one next door to us. The compounding high density was creating a sense of encroachment, a stifling desperation and strangulation, like the endless dust, choking, choking.

Not long after Ebony died, we left too. The owners of the house we had been renting lived abroad, a set of elderly siblings who quarrelled over the fate of the land, and those wanting to sell won. We went somewhere green with wide, open spaces, where the scent of blood was a memory.

The Biggest Fête

It seemed the whole fête was a sea of purple, black, and white. So glad I had gotten that memo in advance, 'cause there I was in the thick of it, lots of black lace at my wrists and neck, puffed out, and a slinky, sheathy purple-and-white swirl dress clinging to my bony backside. I didn't care. I was just so glad that I had made it into the *hottest* fête for the season, and I set about looking for two things — meh friends and liquors!

So many familiar faces in here. It did feel a bit eerie, a lot of déjà vu vibes for sure, but at the same time strangely comforting to be around so many people that I knew, even if I wasn't sure exactly how I knew them.

I spotted Jeremy, a guy I had gone to school with but hadn't seen in years. He didn't look a day older than when we had last seen each other, and of course he was impeccably dressed, as always.

I struggled through the crowd. "*Jeremy!*"

"*Vida!*" he exclaimed, pushing through people to give me the most welcomingest hug ever.

"Oh my god, girl. Look ... at ... *you!*"

"You too! You look amazing!"

A handsome young man sidled up to Jeremy. "Oh, Vida, this is Brian."

Brian stuck out his hand. "Enchanté," he said, smiling wickedly. He side-eyed Jeremy. "Oh *god*, Jeremy, where *do* you know all these *bee-yoo-ti-ful* women from?"

I laughed and thanked him.

Jeremy and I then tried to figure how long it had been since we had seen each other last. Had it really been twenty years? Twenty-three? Incredible.

"Where did you go? After high school it was like you disappeared!" I said.

"Well, I did darling, I diiiiid!"

I watched his face a little more intently now.

"You know high school *was not* the easiest time for me."

I did remember. All the bullying he had had to endure. The nasty notes stuck to his locker. *BULLAHMAN. FAGGOT.* Sharpie drawings of penises inserted into mouths, into bottoms, scribbled on bathroom stalls with the word *JEREMY* clearly underneath. Gay porn pics downloaded from the internet, printed out and masking-taped to his desk. On and on it went — for years.

"Well, you know what they say — the best revenge is living well!"

Jeremy and Brian exchanged looks. Brian shrugged.

I was starting to get thirsty. While we had been talking I had been surreptitiously scanning the room for a bar, but still couldn't see one.

"Where's the bar?" I asked.

Before Jeremy could answer, he did the strangest thing. For a second he kind of shape-shifted into this transparent hologram-type existence, full of light, and then he bent over completely backwards (so that his head was nearly touching his heels) and opened his mouth, and I saw a slip of amber liquid go straight down his throat! This all happened in mere seconds.

He bounced back upright and said "Thanks!" to no one in particular.

"Uhhhh … what the hell was that?" I said.

"Was what?" he asked, staring at me blankly. "Ohhhh right, you're new here! This is how we drink now. Only libations. Offerings to the jumbie. Thank god Caribbean people still keep that tradition alive!"

"My turn!" shouted Brian, raising his hand in an exaggerated way. He, too, bent over backwards, nearly touching the ground with his head, but his limbo dip had way more style, panache, and *finesse* than Jeremy's had. I had to refrain from applauding.

"Wow! That was something!" I exclaimed. "I —"

"Your turn!" they both announced, and with that they each took one of my arms and I felt myself going full-on back, dipping, but as if I had no vertebrae. My mouth involuntarily opened, and what tasted like Vat 19 rum ran down my throat. I gulped it thirstily and came back up.

"Good girl!" said Jeremy, clapping with glee.

"How was it?" asked Brian, resting his chin on his hands in midair, batting his eyelashes, looking like an enraptured schoolgirl.

I didn't know what to say. "Good?"

"All right! Whadja get?"

"I dunno. It tasted like … Vat 19?"

"*Vat?*" they both shouted incredulously.

"Oh, *honey*," said Brian, "you have *got* to upgrade your living to start offering you top shelf!"

My living?

Just then the lights went up on the stage, which was enormous by any standards. In fact, the entire fête was probably the biggest I had ever been in. I could not see where it began or ended. The crowd just seemed to go on and on and on. The MC got up on the stage and the band started up — I mean a real brass band, like back in the day! Wow, I was not expecting this! Great touch! It looked like they were going to start the evening with some old-time calypsonians. Cool, a back-in-time vibe. I could get into this. A nice warm-up before things really got going with the soca that was sure to come.

As the lights on the crowd went down and the spotlight glared on the stage, I started looking around at *how many people* were doing the weird dip-back-and-gulp move. I mean, it seemed every few seconds I saw someone doing this. Then, without warning, it was my turn again. This time, I didn't need Brian or Jeremy to assist me. I recognized the urge when it hit, and I slipped backwards so quickly and with such ease. The *reward* of that liquor sliding down my throat — well! I had no idea liquor could taste *so good*! Not only that, it seemed to go straight to my head more quickly than usual, and I was *flying*, grooving to that old calypso like nobody's business. This may have been because the shot I just gulped? Puncheon! *Wooiiiieee!* My body was feeling no pain, and as I danced, I realized I could move it in amazing and unprecedented ways — I was limber for days!

I dipped back again.

"Say thaaaaank yooooou!" Jeremy sang-shouted in my ear while wining his waist like he had no joints. The band was quite loud.

"Thank youuuu!" I sang as I myself wined in a circle of my own making. *Dis music too sweet, laaaaawwd fadder!* Jeremy and Brian joined in with me, and next thing we were jamming in a sandwich and I was de meat!

I started to laugh at the absurdity of what I was seeing before me, all these people only drinking by bending backwards, not a bar in sight, yet everybody tight. What de aaaaassssss was really taking place?

I spotted a familiar face through the crowd. Allicia! Oh god, but she looking *rell good*! Next ting, our eyes make four. I see her eyebrows shoot up, her mouth open. She started waving excitedly at me, then pushed her way through the crowd. We hugged up tight tight.

"Vidaaa gyal, yuh reach! Yuh really reach!"

"Yes, man, how not? But look at you! Eh eh, you looking rell good!"

And then I remembered that Allicia had died in a car crash many years back.

Hadn't she?

Allicia must have seen the look on my face because she laughed and said, "Wha'appen, yuh seein a ghost?"

"I —"

Before I could respond, there I was backwards over my ass (backasswards in fact), slurping away. The libations were coming hot and heavy now, and it seemed the minute I was upright, I flew back down again to slurp some more. I noticed Allicia was similarly engaged. When the flurry finally seemed to subside, Allicia arranged her coiffure and said, "Oh *lord*, every year this does happen! Four a.m. Jouvert Morning, everyone bustin open dey bottle an trowin 'one fuh de jumbie!'"

I thought of how many Jouvert Mornings I had done just that. Joyous, abandoned, possessed, dutty dutty dutty, and free. Just free, so free, a freeness indescribable. An drunk no mudder C. *Drunk*.

I was beginning to feel the same in this fancy-ass fête. I mean, people were real dressed up, looking nice, smelling nice, but it was clear that people were tight like fuck and also freeing up, jus like those ole Jouvert vibes I thought were long forgotten.

"One fuh de jumbie, indeed!" I laughed.

As if on cue, the MC returned to the stage and announced, "Now the moment you have all been waiting for: the Lord Intruder and … 'Jumbie Jamboree!'"

Wait, what? Intruder? Wait, nuh they have calypso impersonator here too tonight? Wheeyyy!

Eh eh, but he *rell* popular boy! Hear de crowd roar! What de hell!

I see a man get on stage and grab the mic like it was an old lover and start to belt *chune*.

Back to back, belly to belly
Ah dohn care a damn, Ah done dead already,
Back to back, belly to belly,
Was a jumbie jamboree!

The whole place went mad, singing along with the Lord Intruder impersonator, doing the jumbie dance. I threw an arm around Allicia shoulder and we started prancing back and forth to the music, singing at the top of our lungs. Libations continued to feed us, and so everybody head nice. I saw Jeremy and Brian somewhere in the milieu, rubbing deyselves silly all on dey back and belly and belly to back and what not. Was a scene, papa, oui!

The Intruder impersonator carried on, the crowd bringing him back for three encores, three new verses he had to make up on the spot. And he delivered! The crowd was whistling, stamping, jumping, cheering. One man next to me bawl out, "Intruder bwoy! Dat is *kaiso*!"

I laughed, said to Allicia, "Wow, that impersonator rell good, gyal!"

She watched me funny. "Impersonator? But dat is de man self!"

I had to agree. I mean who could have really told this impersonator apart from the real man?

The crowd was so hype as "Intruder" made his departure, I thought, *All we need now is an iron section to keep the vibes going.*

And jus so, who come on de stage but a section beatin fuh dey life, ah setta ole timers, it look like, but — no, some young'uns in de crowd, too! Why did they look so familiar? I must have followed this section at some point at some Jouvert in my lifetime.

The next thing, I spotted The Brothers in the crowd. Like twins, each had on a hard hat but was bareback, with a pure buff-muscled chest and some tight, sexy jeans and construction boots. The Brothers were a scene, a legend. There they went, through the crowd, each one rhythmically hitting the other one's hard hat with a broomstick, while chipping, prancing, palancing to de iron rhythm. It was *sweeeeet*, fuh so. People turned to watch their impromptu performance, and then I recognized others in the crowd engaged in similar ole mas. Flagman, another Carnival institution, waving he flag as if he life depended on it, furious with it, his face so serious, but so artful with his dips and dives and swooshes. And Mama, who had sewn endless Carnival costumes for children and adults alike, her arms fully extended, prancing four steps forward, four steps back, four steps forward, four steps back, but her face a mask, entranced. You *knew* this woman was a seasoned Queen of the Band! Finally, Bell Man emerged from the throng, energetically waving the Baptist school bell high above the heads of the celebrants, giving it all he had, awakening the spirits, the spirits of the —

I heard a chant rumbling through the crowd in response to the sweet sweet iron, the "engine room" as David Rudder had dubbed it, the heartbeat of a nation. *"Lighters up!"* I kept hearing. *"Lighters up, lighters up!"* My head was bad; I wanted to tie it up in a red cloth and let Changó take over, but something kept me dancing dancing dancing, chipping, swaying, arms crossing in and out, in and out, *"Lighters up!"* but no one was lighting a damn thing, just the endless beating of that iron and then a *whiiiiiisstlle* cutting through that rhythm, a whistle to mess up yuh head even badder, achuggachugga achuggachugga achuggachugga chug chug chug chugchugchugchug chugchug *tweeeeeeeeeeeeeeet!*

"*Lighters up! Lighters up!*"

Then something shifted for me and I heard what everyone was really saying: "*Light … us … up!*"

And jus so, a wave of flickering lights began to materialize through the crowd, hovering just above everyone's heads, small but beautiful illuminations, candle flames without the candles, mysterious tiny firefly flickers floating in the darkness, suspended above and around people's heads. How stunning! Some people were simply blotted out by the intensity and sheer numbers of flames I saw crowning them, while others only had one or two flickers of light above them. And then I saw blurry colours above the lights, fuzzy faces, people's features moving as if through a lens focusing and unfocusing, an image dissolving and reassembling itself. And the people in the crowd to whom these images were connected by some mysterious force began to smile and wave and dance and extend their arms upwards to these faces in welcome and recognition. *I see you. Thank you for remembering me. I love you. We love you. Gone but not forgotten. I am fine. We are fine. I miss you. I miss you too.*

My head must have been *rell* bad because I, too, thought I saw lights flickering above me, around me, like intense beaming butterflies. And as if looking through the bottom of a cut-crystal glass full of whisky, I was seeing glimpses of people: my two sisters, my dad, James, my co-workers? Janice from church? What de hell? More and more and more faces materializing and blurring in the dark, vague. Peter, my first boyfriend from secondary school. Our neighbours the Redmans from my childhood house in Woodbrook …

Where were *you*?

I felt myself being lifted off the ground ever so slightly, ever so gently, and my arms began to rise. And I felt bliss washing over me. Bliss, joy, peace — every good and righteous feeling was washing over me, like bright, warm sunshine after a cold, damp rain.

This amazing feeling grew and deepened and intensified, and I could see, from my slightly elevated position, that everyone's lights were connecting; the fête had become like a highway of light, like watching the East-West Corridor at night from a plane window when your flight is coming in for a landing, first low over the black shadows of the Northern Range, then *bam!*, one long string of lights, street lights, highway lights, headlights, tail lights, all shimmering, flowing in an illuminated river. They had *not* forgotten us! I understood, at last. We had kept this tradition alive enough in our country so that we, those of us now here, could still fête and dance and wine and laugh and sing and be at peace. Maybe we weren't at the level of the Mexicans with their Día de los Muertos, or the Haitians with their Fête Guede, but we still had All Souls Day. And we had Jouvert.

I also realized in that moment that this fête was so big because so many were qualifying early to attend this damn all-inclusive — ha! — this *all-inclusive* party. Wasn't no setta exclusively old people in here! Had anyone really run down tickets to this fête? Had *I*? I wasn't even sure yet how I had reach here in the first place! So many here were obviously premature patrons, in attendance for totally unnatural reasons. I was beginning to recognize people's faces more and more, but not from my own circle — from grainy newspaper photos, the seven o'clock news, from front page headlines decrying a rising murder rate, a horrific crime scene, road carnage. These patrons were here having a time after *not* having lived out a full, long life. Nope.

The iron section began to peter out, and little by little the intensity of the millions of tiny lights began to subside. The party patrons relaxed, began to converse with each other again, and the images of their loved ones slowly dissipated into the darkness. The DJ was back in action on the turntable, blasting some classic Carnival soca chunes. It was a bittersweet moment. My heart suddenly ached. I missed you. Why hadn't I seen you amongst the others when the lights surrounded me? Had you really forgotten me? I now knew where I was, but I didn't know how I had gotten here. Who gave me the damn ticket?

Rupee was belting out about how everyone needed to enjoy themselves now, in this mas, in this fête, cuz no one knows what tomorrow will bring.

More libations were being offered with this number, and we resumed our bending and slurping. I felt to cry. Were our living hearing the same music we were?

And then, there you were. You encircled my waist from behind, and I felt the familiar press of your body against my backside, the full of my back, your arms now wrapping around me, snugly, rocking me to the rhythm. I didn't dare turn around, but I could smell your cologne and your body scent, and I instinctively reached my hand up to slide it along your neck and touch your ear and then your hair. Despite the years, my fingers knew that path intimately, every curve of your neck, your jaw, your cheek, every hair of your beard. It *was* you! It was really you. I was overwhelmed with joy, joy so intense it was nearly choking me, but I let myself float in the high of the music and the rhythm we were so perfectly rocking to: Nadia Batson's "So Long," the sweetest reunion, the fear of loss quelled by the reappearance of that long-lost love.

You never let go as we rocked together for song after song after song, our hips in perfect sync. I did not know if hours or days passed; time was impossible to measure anymore. I do know at some point — just as with every Jouvert — the inklings of dawn began to appear in the sky, that greyish hue, and then a light, wispy blue, becoming more and more intense, until finally the sun burst through, crimson and tangerine and golden honey, and the sweet shadows of the night became delineated realities in the harsh morning light. More and more people started disappearing from the fête, dissolving, evaporating, fading out. As their living

sobered up, headed home, or passed out, dutty, tired, oblivious, so
too we had to melt away. I didn't even bother to turn around when
the pressure of your delicious body was no longer there. I knew
there was an eternity waiting for us, and then I, too, disappeared
on myself.

I's de Man Lane

Here we are again. I instinctively clutch the door handle, not the one that opens the door, but the one you can grip without fear of a door flying open and pelting you on the roadway. My pulse accelerates, my breathing deepens. I am tense. Muscles clenching, I secretly pray that I can survive what is about to happen.

I feel that he feels the tension too. The car begins to speed up. *Oh no.* I can feel his impatience — with the other drivers, with the potholes, with the badly patched roadway, layers upon layers of tar just heaped up haphazardly without a care over years, beaten down by endless cars and trucks and maxi taxis. He wants to avoid these bumps, these potential damagers of vehicles that can send you to the mechanic's to pelt out thousands of dollars after your car mash up.

Cheeupsss.

He's sucking his teeth. Fuck.

All of a sudden the car lurches into the middle lane. The No Man's Lane. The *I's de Man* Lane. *Who is de bigger man, Papi?* For a stretch of a few miles, some bright star decided that there should be a "sometimeish" lane, a third lane, a middle lane in between two designated, stable, sane lanes, one that flows east and one that flows west. For half the day, from morning rush hour, the direction of the middle lane flows west, into the city. By midafternoon, the direction switches to east, carrying commuters out of the city. There are signposts staggered along the length of this roadway to explain the lane's transdirectional nature. But this is Trinidad. Since when people read sign? Since when people follow rule? Rule is meant to be broken! *I's de man!*

There are no cars ahead of us. This should be good, right? Well, no. It just means that if we meet whatever might be coming toward us, we will get it head-on. No buffer car to take the brunt.

What the hell is *that* ahead?

"No no no no no! Oh god, just get out of this lane! Please!"

I can't take it. I am having visions of head-on collisions. This is anathema to me. The absolute definition of instability and chaos. Anybody in this middle earth could claim *I's de man! De fockin man, oui!* Who am I? A small woman at the mercy of all this testosterone.

He is oblivious to my pleas. The more I whimper, the more he barrels down the road, as if his grand charge will dominate any and all competitors. Freakin gladiator sports at 2:30 p.m. on the Eastern Main Road.

A giant silver Hilux is coming at us like a locomotive. I don't know what time it is anymore. I don't know what the rules of this lane are. Does it matter? Does Mr. Hilux really give a damn? Or is this a battle to the death? Who will chicken out first and move into "their" lane? This is madness. I suck in my breath sharply and squeeze my eyes shut. I feel sick. It is terrifying.

Hilux nearly runs a red Corolla off the road to squeeze into "his" lane at the last minute. I guess we are within our rights. I guess the gods are favouring us.

Now I have to listen to a tirade. "Why are you such a *coward*? Why don't you trust my driving?"

More madness. I am mute.

Where are the women, I wonder? Do they also take charge of this strip of asphalt at times and haul ass, barrelling into a future unknown? Do they throw down the automotive gauntlet and test their luck? Do they drive as if they are in a life-size game of *Grand Theft Auto*, giving the finger to the world, the police, god, the government, and fellow drivers?

Or are they like me, a huddled mass of cortisol, feeling the years sheared from their lifespans from the stress of having to endure this, day in, day out, this relentless three thousand metres of poor urban planning, while some man behind the wheel plots his revenge on any and all drivers who apparently represent his past wounds and present traumas and frustrations. *I's de man, boy!* The speed demons, the entitled mama's boys who cannot take a no, not from anyone; the wealthy princes in sleek, expensive cars; the teenage boys who feel immortal; the wannabe gangsters who have their back up at all times, all routinely testing out their manhood in this blasted middle lane.

One morning, a big trailer truck, moving in the same direction that we were headed, tried to squeeze us out of the middle lane. It just kept coming and coming and coming at my passenger door, and we were in the middle lane, and there was nowhere to go. No. Where. To. Go. We could have headed straight into oncoming traffic to avoid being squished by this big truck. But no. *I's de man* just stopped the car. Turned off the engine. Jumped out of the driver's seat. Went to the cab of the trailer truck. Opened the door of the driver's side and — *whap whap* — hit the man two calpet in he head. "Yuh chupid? Eh? Is kill yuh tryin to kill we? Eh? Yuh muddercunt!"

Back in the car and down the road we went. I remember thinking, *Now he is really enraged*. At times like this I feel a critical mass
of adrenalin rising up between my stomach and my diaphragm. I
feel I may vomit. I wonder if that would also anger him. I fantasize
about suddenly flinging my door open and dive-rolling out the car
like a stunt extra on a Hollywood set, breaking my fall skillfully
with a tuck 'n' roll. But I know the reality of that happening is very
slim, and I would end up as a puddled mass of blood and gore by
the side of the road. I cling to the door handle instead, my usual
go-to security blanket, and hold on for dear life.

The thing is there's *I's de man*s all over this island. You see
them daily in the newspaper, on social media, on nightly television
newscasts. "21-year-old of Santa Cruz ...," "43-year-old father of
five ...," "Coast Guard officer, 39 ...," "Anthony Speckles, also
known as 'Speck,' apparently lost control of his vehicle. ..." Where?
Where? Tell me it's the *I's de Man* Lane where this occurred! Please
vindicate me so that he will know I am not mad, I am not a coward
or paranoid but a *sane, sane* person in an insane society. Barrelling
down an insane stretch of road in a country going to hell in a
handbasket. *Tell him.*

"*Fuck!*"

He's overtaking the car ahead of us by utilizing this middle
road of hell but the *car headlights coming toward us are far too* —

Back out. He's back in the left lane. My life is intact. I have all
my limbs still, my eyesight. Thank god.

At first, I began to bargain with the *I's de Man* Lane. "Just
bring me a dead. Jus one. I want to *show* him how dangerous this
game is. How crucial the stakes are."

But the lane would not cooperate. I tried to appease Ogun,
Yoruban god of the road, of accidents, of bloodshed, of cars. Nothing
doing. Not even a dog carcass did I see by the side of the road. Nada.

He told me I should learn to drive. That I can't tell him anything, I cannot critique unless I am willing to take the wheel and

handle mehself. Maybe there is a metaphor in that. Maybe I am not really living, maybe I need to face death every day like he does, gauging inches and milliseconds that would determine mine — or another person's — life expectancy. Maybe I need to be that bold and reckless. After all, what does tomorrow hold?

The murder rate is going to surpass 450 again this year, I just know it. I'm not sure how many of those murders are the result of anger gone awry, "crimes of passion," and how many may be just pure blood sacrifice. I don't know exactly who is doing it, who is behind all this, but when you see people's throats being slit and then left to bleed out … well, that is blood sacrifice, isn't it? Some people say the current prime minster working Tobagonian obeah and others saying the former prime minister was pouring milk from state helicopters onto Hindu statues, so who really knows?

When I see someone driving mad on the road, it crosses my mind — did they recently walk in on a family member's body, red with blood, bludgeoned to a pulp, or like a sieve full of bullet holes? Are they still lighting candles and praying for a loved one who simply vanished, into thin air apparently, no body recovered? Was their son or husband or brother gunned down in a hail of bullets, by men or boys who looked just like him? Were the killers men who are supposed to "protect and serve"?

You bury your loved one, or you don't bury them because they cannot find a corpse, or maybe it isn't a corpse; maybe your loved one was shipped out and is alive but suffering somewhere in human bondage, and this you will never know.

You get in your car every day like a robot, drive mindlessly, recklessly, secretly hoping that someone will just snuff out your life, anything to make the pain and emptiness stop.

The hopelessness that people here cannot speak about. They get in their cars and just drive, drive. Some have to drive. Some choose to drive. They drive as if they don't give a damn; they drive to forget. Like they are taunting death: *Take me nah!*

If this is true, then maybe the *I's de Man* Lane is a portal. Maybe all the roads of Trinidad are holy gateways, merciful angels of death, designed like the steam vent of a pressure cooker to expel the tension, balance things out, prevent total catastrophe. A concrete corbeaux clean-up crew.

Today I sit in the car. This time I'm mute. There is nothing more to be said. I accept the chaos that I find myself in — the small one in this car, on this road, and the larger one no one wants to talk about. One way or another, my life could be snuffed out at any time. Stray bullet. Home invasion. Robbery. Innocent bystander. Mistaken identity. Bad drive.

Maybe this is the divine plan after all. Maybe this actually *makes sense.*

Mr. Bull's Garden

There was a tiny wishing well in the midst of this verdant jungle. At least to Terra's five-year-old eyes it *looked* like a tiny wishing well, and to her five-year-old stature it *seemed* like a jungle. The growing season was so short, and it was only in May that the whole yard would fill out in a covering of crawlers, moss, bluebells, lilies of the valley, and other plants that loved the dank, dark moistness of a forest floor. By September the show would be over, and she would have to wait it out until the miracle of spring again brought out the crocuses, trumpeting narcissus, and the harbingers of true spring in May: lilies of the valley.

Mr. Bull's garden had been Terra's haven ever since her mother allowed her to wander into the neighbour's backyard by herself. She would crawl through an open part of the fence that separated their house from his and enter the land of enchantment. Her first stop would be the tiny wishing well, sculpted by Mr. Bull's hands, she was sure, a tiny vessel of stones and cement that held rainwater and dew and served as a bird bath for passing sparrows, sometimes a robin. She would circle the well chanting her wishes, all the while dropping offerings into the water — honeysuckle flowers, leaves, and twigs she had imbued with some mystical potency — and wait for the water nymphs and fairies to spirit away her requests.

Sometimes she would spy Mr. Bull watching her mildly through his back door. He was a very old, very White man. He never spoke to her, never chased her off his property, and honestly did not seem to mind the two little brown girls from next door traipsing through his garden almost daily.

Mr. Bull clearly loved flowers, as he planted several rows of bold tulips and plebeian geraniums in his front yard. But she never wandered through that neat, sanitary plantation with its flowers lined up like soldiers in military formation. The front yard flowers were on display; all passersby and cars that swept down the tree-lined street could see them, as Mr. Bull did not have very thick hedges bordering his yard. It was all too open and too exposed. She was drawn instead to that wildness behind his house, the riotous greenery that threatened to overtake even the venerable oak and maple trees which stood like black sentinels, watching over the power of the place. There was something *in* there that drew her back again and again. And even though her sister accompanied her often, and they would both walk around and around the cobbled wishing well as if performing some ancient ritual, she knew her sister did not have the patience to listen and understand the true depth of the garden, to hear the messages that came when raindrops fell elegantly on wide-open emerald leaves, so delicate and fragile, so bursting with life, as if knowing that their brief appearance would be cut short by a Manitoba frost all too soon, the frigid November, the kiss of death.

In the wintertime there was nowhere to conjure the spirits, nowhere to connect with the hum of photosynthesis, the drinking of nectar by bees, the reverberation of raindrops falling into the occult wishing well. The garden became white. Just white. Fully blanketed in blinding snow, it would disappear beneath this shroud for many months, heap upon heap of soft and flakey, then hard and impenetrable, iced and crusty, pure white snow. Once in a while she would glimpse Mr. Bull shovelling his front walkway — no scarlet geraniums now to herald the borders of his property — and she wondered what he did all winter.

In time she came of age to attend kindergarten, and even though the smell of books had excited her for some time now, school was both a pleasure and a curse. By grade one Terra was marked apart as an exceptionally bright child. Learning intoxicated her, as did her grade-one teacher's perfume and the beautiful flowering plants — African violets, Christmas cacti, and angel wing begonias — that her teacher tended on the windowsill. Although Terra made lots of friends, she knew school was not safe. It was not safe to be on the concrete playground when boys were restless and might suddenly turn on her with spotlight taunts aimed at her skin colour. She then realized it was not safe to show the teachers how bright she was, how good a reader she was, how big a vocabulary she had, because one day the principal plucked her, like a rare blossom, out of the classroom with the warm, loved beehive hairdo of her pompadoured, perfumed teacher and put her in a class of older students with whom she felt afraid and muted, even paralyzed. The teacher in that class had a line for a mouth, stiff wire-rimmed glasses, and a shag haircut; she was starchy, clipped. The classroom windowsill was lined with clay flowerpots holding nothing but shrivelled, dead plants. Terra longed for the simplicity of her life before school. The quiet time with her mother at home, watching TV while her mother ironed the laundry, or the moments when she could concoct her spells in Mr. Bull's garden. Now she had to contend. Now she had to defend herself. She developed stomach migraines.

As the years passed the unpleasantness of school only worsened. No matter how many chants Terra prayed over the peashrub leaves she assiduously plucked off delicate stems during her walks home from school, counting, counting, hoping for a magical conjuring that could protect her, she had lost some of that otherworldly connection, the mystic she had been able to conjure while circling the tiny wishing well in her childhood, chanting and dropping floral offerings. She did not have a word for this state of being, but she knew something was missing.

Her parents couldn't help her. They, too, had lost any connections they might have once had with land and plants and water, wind and rain, in a prior era, a different vibratory age. They were caught up in their own traumas. Her father felt the sting of indifference in the boys' world of the office, where his Caribbean accent and skin brown as rich earth meant being overlooked and ridiculed; this raised his pressure and he would come home at lunchtime to lie on the couch, popping prescribed pills that changed his personality. Terra's mother, relegated to housewifery, turned herself inside out in acts of self-sacrifice to the altar of the family, endlessly cooking and cleaning, burying her resentment in her body like tulip bulbs that eventually emerged as cancerous nuggets in her breasts.

As Terra approached puberty, one by one her friends withered away. Her best friend, Patricia, announced one day that she would no longer be coming to Terra's house after school as had been the norm. Terra's mom called Patricia's mom, and after a tense exchange, Terra's mom hung up the phone. Not quite knowing how to explain to her daughter what had transpired, she simply said, "Those people are ignorant." Later, Terra overheard her mother explaining to her father that Patricia's mother did not want her daughter associating with a "half-breed." Terra didn't quite understand, but she had the same feeling in her stomach as when she was singled out in the playground by the taunting boys. Always something about her body; always something about her brownness.

Frank (the equally Aryan son of a city councillor), had always been the boy to her girl, her male counterpart, both of them bright, curious students, he with his sun-freckled skin, cornflower eyes, and wheat-coloured hair, and she with her cinnamon skin, mahogany eyes, and pitch-black hair. Now it seemed Frank had abandoned her as well. Terra had invited him to her eleventh birthday party along with all the other children, as she had since grade one, but this year he suddenly "forgot." When Frank never arrived on her doorstep for the one o'clock party (as the other invitees had), Terra's mother telephoned Frank's mother. The carload of children then had to swing by Frank's house on the way to the play park to pick him up; in the car he absentmindedly handed Terra an old board game casually wrapped in newspaper — her birthday gift. She felt herself evaporating right there, like a raindrop on hot asphalt.

By grade six, other girls — not her, not cinnamon-skinned Terra — became popular with the boys in her class, these blue-eyed, milk-fed boys, who increasingly did not notice her, even to taunt her as they used to. She became, without warning, inexplicably invisible. At first Terra danced and danced a fine tightrope on a silken strand trying to appease this one and that one, trying to find the magic potion that would win the love of the sun-freckled, cornflower-eyed boys, hoping that their recognition would elevate her, give her wings, and allow her to embrace her burgeoning power. But their gazes lay elsewhere.

Terra was so focused on this loss of recognition that she forgot to notice the shifting axis of the Earth, the equinoxes, the migration of birds, the buds forming, and the leaves falling. She now scoffed at her once daily practice of, one by one, loosing the teardrop-shaped peashrub leaves from their tender twigs as she chanted, "He loves me, he loves me not, he loves me, he loves me not," ecstatic when the last leaf cast from her hand indicated *he loves me*. Her stomach migraines worsened; she lost weight. Where there should have been fullness and abundance, she was withering on the vine.

In the midst of all this, Mr. Bull died.

She didn't know when it happened, and heard about it later from her mother. A white ambulance had come to take him away, a stretcher. She didn't absorb the details. For her, the magic of that childhood garden was all but forgotten. For her, life had become a perpetual winter, a daily brutality, cutting down and annihilating what had once been lush foliage, curious honeybees, the promise of renewal in a tiny sprout. Similarly, Mr. Bull's garden was razed to make way for the new neighbours and their vista: some kind of treated cedar walkway and trellis-like design of little character, with composite decking. The black oaks perished shortly thereafter.

When spring finally did return, and the boys suddenly took a renewed interest in Terra, it was only to gaze upon her budding form, her slight curves and developing roundness. They feigned interest in her romantically as a guise to get at her body, their fingers digging into her like pickaxes, running up and down her legs like tractors, overturning her clothes like plows making furrows in the dirt. Still she allowed them this, opening her face, her heart, her hands, opening, opening, allowing and permitting, abiding and inert. She had their recognition, but soon realized it was not this she wanted or needed. These same boys did not grab and grope at the blond-haired girls who looked like their sisters, their mothers, their aunts. There was no sealed cloak, no magic potion to make the cornflower-eyed boys love her — more importantly, to make them respect her.

Grade six graduation. The gymnasium decorated in a tropical theme: palm trees, coconuts, and big, red, lascivious crepe-paper hibiscus suspended from the ceiling. A boy she liked was point-ing her out to his father. She came closer, as their smiles seemed inviting. This boy had tried to kiss her once behind the piano at assembly, forcefully, hands groping clumsily, tugging at her cowl-necked sweater. Someone had seen, and the news burned through the school like a raging fire, tainting her. As she approached the two, she overheard the father, leering and smiling and sweating, say to his son "Got yourself a little jungle bunny, eh?" She wanted to disappear behind the palm trees, dissolve and be transported by the red hibiscus spaceships. She wanted to flee.

Terra was left completely to her own devices: no parents, teach-ers, guidance counsellors, or friends could help her. The spirits she had been unconsciously hoping would save her began to take up residence in her head. She mounted her bike each day as if a steed; she rode her bike everywhere, far away from people, talking to it and treating it as a horse, and chanting as she pumped the pedals, opening herself to forces both good and evil, because there were no elders to guide her otherwise.

One day she took hold of this chant: *Hail Mary, full of grace, the Lord is with thee. Blessed art thou amongst women, and blessed is the fruit of thy womb, Jesus.* She didn't know how the chant arrived in her mouth. It had jumped out of her head into her mouth and now captured her in a rapturous rhythm as she pumped the pedals. Terra had never been in a Roman Catholic church. She had never attended a Mass. And yet there it was — *Hail Mary.* The stomach migraines eased. The tears reduced. She cared less about the boys at school and their blond-haired cohorts. The change was subtle, but there. The power of the word. Aşe in her lengua.

She picked up books again, spiritual books this time, esoteric ones, ones written by and for the elders. She found herself drawn more frequently to the forests that lined the massive rivers cut-ting through the city, the two mighty serpentine forces that met and melded and synergized, and all along their banks were hidden copses and emerald respites. She would go there and pray, not familiar with the words that seemed to emanate from her mouth without her bidding. She became interested in fire and found herself igniting conflagrations randomly, fascinated by the power and the energy that could both destroy and be extinguished in an instant. Tinkering with these elements, communicating with them, became a central practice.

As her energy rose, and she connected more and more with her inner power, her life in the outer world conversely became more dangerous. It was as if she was giving out a new scent, strong as night-blooming jasmine, a scent that attracted all kinds of creatures. One day, while she was in one of her forest reveries, a man appeared. She froze. Like a deer startled by the sudden presence of a hunter, she was on high alert. *Get out.* Too late. He was close enough now that she could breathe in his heavy stink scent of old, sour beer and unbrushed teeth and cigarettes. When he tried to grab her, she began to scream, gouging his eyes, kicking him as hard as her twelve-year-old feet would allow. He released her.

Not every green space was Mr. Bull's garden. Not every man would watch her mildly. She retreated again.

In time she met like-minded outcasts, those who were equally drawn to the riverbanks and bonfires and the boundaries of society. She felt safety in this herd. These beings introduced her to ganja, and she found a whole new way to communicate with the spirits. She spent the latter half of her adolescence in a haze of smoke, eager to feel that relaxation, her mind expanding, losing herself in the music, the healing plant, the holy and sacred herb of Hindus and Rastas. This helped her survive the countdown. Terra was a minor who was beholden to parents and the law and teachers and society. She was not yet in a place where she could determine her own life. So she puffed away daily on a homemade chillum, seeking escape through the music and the herb and her dreams of a life post-eighteen: adulthood and emancipation.

Terra dreamt of the ability to escape the winters and the cold and the snow and the whiteness. She dreamt of the Caribbean, where her ancestors were from; she dreamt of verdant mountains, covered from top to bottom with thick, dense foliage that never abated, even in the dry season; she fantasized about cascades of torrential rain and hazy blue clouds descending on the emerald mountaintops, and healing herbs and plants abounding all around her. She saw herself there. She was determined to get there. She knew it was the only chance she had — to get out and get there and be finally healed in the embrace of Amazonian forest. Bob Marley and Culture, Bunny Wailer and Burning Spear, all singing and chanting about Babylon (the oppressor) and Zion (the Promised Land). To her Zion was not Africa, but a tiny island in the Caribbean where her predecessors' bones were buried, Iere, Land of the Hummingbird. She was going to Zion.

•

TERRA CONTINUED IN HER ESOTERIC STUDIES, SCHOOLING herself in alternate energies to survive the interim. Crystals, herbal medicine, chanting, flower-essence remedies. She left her parents' home, changed cities, changed boyfriends; changed jobs, changed hairstyles and clothes and friends — but still the persecution remained. It was all around her. The looks when she went to rent a place. The raised eyebrows when she went to apply for a job. When she enrolled in university, security guards followed her in the hallways, or asked her for ID. Some of her classmates ostracized her in the same way the blue-eyed, blond-haired tribe had done in primary school. Her professors found her too angry, dismissed her work as "too political." In her Creative Writing 101 class, she composed a poem that, to her, was the sharpened diamond point of all her experiences to date, all the anger and pain and hurt coalesced into a single finite gem, and she titled her obra "Marshmallow

Lynching" to signify the soft, White, cushy way that Canadian racism manifested. You could try punching back, attacking, pushing, shoving, impaling — but all you would get was a bounce back of puffy, bland ineffectualness, a feigned smile, skin teeth, apologies, denials.

> I pelt my fists, again and again,
> but the foam is too thick,
> I cannot see my enemy.
> My anger spent;
> Pillsbury Doughboy in a cloud.
> But when my efforts finally do connect,
> they are strangely cushioned
> by an infinity of cotton-batting lies.
> Your ivory teeth, blizzards of deception,
> envelop and blind me.

Her professor was incensed, told her this was *not* poetry and that she should enroll in political science instead. He gave "Marshmallow Lynching" a D. She resubmitted a heartfelt poem about Mr. Bull's garden and received an A.

The university classrooms overwhelmed Terra, ensconced as they were within brutalist, monolithic grey cement walls. The institution was built like a medieval fortress. On some days, especially during the winter months, she felt the walls would come crashing down around her, the huge slabs of grim concrete crushing her. The concrete was interposed with some struggling ivy during the warmer months, challenging the monotone ever so slightly. Perhaps if this ivy were brave enough, Terra thought, it could find the cracks in these slabs and push push push, riotously overwhelming the crevices, and blast the concrete apart. She longed for green. Where was the lushness of life, livity, vibration, healing?

Amidst the imposing sterility of the fortress, she discovered a hidden pond. Like a hopeless moat, it contained bulrushes and

birds and a few ducks, with the buzz of insects and the peeping
of frogs. She would flee to this tiny oasis in a valiant attempt to
reconnect with nature, with the enormous vibration of life itself.
The classmate's comment, the professor's insensitivity, a passage in
a book, or a scene in a film: these could ignite a fiery rage within
her, make her brain disconnect and throw her into a conflagration
of turmoil. But concrete walls do not burn. As she had once done
as a child, she retreated to the pond, chanting, circling, throwing
offerings to the stagnant water full of tadpoles and minnows.

At least in the university there were books, to which she again
retreated. Books were the key that opened the gates to esoteric
knowledge, books could help make sense of her dreams, connect
the dots from sensory vibration to dream messages to lived realities. Terra voraciously devoured books and developed a level
of knowledge in many areas of arcane wisdom. She read during
and between the changes to her body that eventual motherhood
brought — roundness, firmness, lushness, liquidness, tiredness,
flaccidness — and the comings and goings of men who wooed
and comforted and attacked and hurt and lied and healed and
pleasured and inflicted pain, and the years trod on. She read in
the absence of elders.

Fully mature Terra found the ways to connect the dots. It had
taken her years to figure out the right methods, the dust of wood
shavings mixed with nature's sacrifices — leaves, roots, flowers,
seeds, fruits, bark — pollinating her dreams with desires and
manifesting outcomes. In the multiple dwelling spaces afforded
her — small or expensive, old or brand new, but never *hers* — she
had always managed to grow something. Basil or tulsi, daisies for
bathing and for offering, parsley, calabazas, mint/mente, Spanish
thyme and siempre viva/wonder of the world, verbena, sunflowers,
even at times hibiscus and gardenias, and then lengua de vaca
and croton for protection. As she moved from ripeness to the ze-
nith of full life force, Terra began to mature and harden. By now

the spirits were seated in her head, enthroned. They proceeded to guide her to her own garden, in the land of her ancestors. She finally escaped to Zion.

Terra meticulously planned every corner of that garden; the way the light fell at certain times of day, where shade would be for shade plants, how to fence off the sacred spaces so the dogs would not violate. She needed special groves for her energies. It would be magnificent. In the middle of it all, she constructed a small stone pond with a miniature fountain, and every morning she would sit outside and watch the birds bathing in it. The garden was the culmination of her life, her offering to the earth. It would take years and years to manifest, but as it did, she wanted it more and more to be the place where she would live out her days, wilt, shrivel up, and then die. She wanted to grow old in this garden, to water many seasons, those that she had left, and then pass away and leave only her shadow behind. Her one regret was that she would not be able to leave her bones there as well, to fertilize the soil and enrich the life busting out and blooming and beholding the earth.

Ghosts of La Rampa

I can see you here now, walking, striding, maybe you have shoes, maybe you don't. Buffed bronze and so full of yourself, a spectre even then, strutting down La Rampa like all the young cocks eyein up each other and eyein up the extrañeros who are eyein up you. You didn't give a damn. Man, woman, it was all the same, just to get the fulas and have something to eat, something nice to wear perhaps, maybe buy some food for mami, drink some Havana Club. You had learned the lingo from pirated hip hop cassettes and were always trying to impress whatever turista came along, showing off your moves — hip hop, timba, son, rumba. It was the nineties and only by a miracle you were surviving. You contemplated the balsa as well; even in the countryside your mother was secretly preparing an old inner tube to get out and make a break for Miami, sharks be damned. But instead an ancient Eurotrash maricon wooed you away to his resort in the Bahamas (so you said). I don't even want to think about what you got up to there. You always downplayed this shit, and who knows? You were slick enough that maybe it was true you got away with this charade for a few weeks without having to fuck his tiny, wrinkled colonial behind, or let his no-lips mouth suck your pinga. But then again, maybe all that did happen.

When your cousin took me to the Tumba Abandonada in El Colón cemetery, I understood a lot better about all of you. The necessity of myth so strong in a place that makes giants out of peasants, the whole David-and-Goliathness of this place. Unafraid to take on anything — the Spanish, the Americans, the Mafia, the Russians, poverty, hunger, need, want, starvation, and death itself. There are so many shadows here, and the shadows are more alive than the living, I always say. As long as one can make peace with the shadows, appease them, feed them, placate them, you will be all right in this place. But if one ignores them, scorns them, ridicules them, if one forgets to lay flores y dulces on the Tumba Abandonada, well, muchacho! (as you would say), I so sorry for joo.

Everybody had to figure out how to resolver, how to get over, how to survive. Your family befriended an old negra in Miramar, an old lady who had one of those beautiful, crumbling villas that persisted as a reminder of a middle class that had once profited off and thoroughly enjoyed Havana the brothel. I don't know how this negra had ended up with this amazing piece of property, but your family was determined to take it out from under her nose, before or after she croaked. Of course, they were outsmarted by this woman's grandchildren, who had gotten wind of some kind of subterfuge and managed to haul their asses from Hialeah and head back to this puta country to resolver again! They invested a bunch of money in upgrading the place and are now whoring it out on Airbnb. What goes around comes around.

(In another scenario, your cousin befriended an old blan-
quita who had a penthouse apartment down the street from the
Nacional. This time your sister made sure that la blanca didn't have
any heirs. She took la doña into her humble home and used her
hard-earned revolutionary skills as a nurse to make herself indis-
pensable to la blanca. In the end, her ruse still didn't work — the
state confiscated the apartment after la blanca's death because her
long-dead husband had been some important member of the party
and it was really state property anyway and blah blah blah. Let's
just say capitalism didn't win that round. Although I swear I saw
that same penthouse being whored out on Airbnb. Must be the
new ministerial hustle — who knows?)

   I don't know if during your time here, before your imminent
and permanent exile, you fathered a few children, because I *swear*
there are times when I am walking to the cadeca, or the open-
air market, or even to catch a taxi, that I see the same face/body
and ass of you walking not four metres ahead of me — by the
Capitolio, on Obispo Street, or running through the avenues of
Vedado as you must have once upon a time. And I wonder, what
has changed? Just like you, these mulattos are grinding a sexy hustle out of the concrete; they are padding the pavement and wearing tight tight clothes and seducing man, woman, or dog to eat a
food. Only now the pickings are much more abundant — with
the two-million-plus tourists descending on this blessed isle yearly,
with every second solar being turned into an "authentic," "retro,"
"colonial-modern" Airbnb, there is so much more to choose from.
So I wonder if these young men, these sons of mambises and
Changó, if they choose men before women, choose men because
it's men they desire, choose women because it's bollo they want, or
does the dollar still decide? These are the things I think about as I
sip my cafecito and watch the world go by on La Rampa, during
the day or at night, sometimes thinking about you but more often
actively not.

I met Antonio in one of those cafés on a rainy afternoon. I was minding my business, sipping the cafecito and eating a piece of flan, when he came into the place like a maelstrom, five feet ten inches of solid man; long, curly hair and hyped-up muscles; strangely plucked or waxed eyebrows; skin-tight clothes showing off every bulge necessary; and a gold Santa Barbara medallion *swanging* on his chest. His eyes passed over me nonchalantly because, like most Cubans, he read me as one of his own, and therefore of no interest. He was chasing fulas. I admit I kept glancing back at him because he was such a pappyshow mélange of characters that I was intrigued and trying to figure out what he was actually up to.

He climbed up on one of the bar stools and started chatting away — loudly — with the bartender and servers. They answered him back with equal gusto; it was clear he was a regular here and everyone was tight. Feeing bored, I decided to play a little game. I walked up to the counter where he was sitting and beckoned the bartender, then ordered a mojito (the ubiquitous touristy drink) in perfect English, asking "How much?" just to up the ante. I could feel Antonio's eyes burning into me as he now sized me up a little bit differently.

Five minutes later he was by my table asking (in heavily accented English) if I could take a picture of him and the staff with his cellphone. He said it was to send to his girlfriend in Canada. "Joo know Canada?"

I told him yes, of course, I *was* Canadian!

"Joo Canadian?" he exclaimed, excited now.

"Sí."

He pulled up a chair instantly, turned it around so he could lean on the back of it, and spread his heavily muscled thighs across the breadth of the seat. "My girfren, she live in Whitby. Joo know Whitby?"

I told him *yes*. He told me how he was waiting on a ticket to go and visit her. How he expected to stay up there for three, four months. If he liked it — who knows? — maybe he might stay for good! Get married, settle down, have a few children. Send for his mami. (I imagined his mami had probably orchestrated this whole "relationship," but I kept that perspective to myself.) He asked me if it was my first time in Havana. I lied.

My mojito arrived and the games began. How long was I staying in Cuba for? Had I visited any of the tourist sites? El Morro? El Catedral? El Floridita? La Gran Hotel Manzana Kempinski (not exactly a tourist site, but I knew where he was going with this — he would have made you proud, the hustle he was trying to hustle on me). I answered *no* to each one. His eyes lit up. He smiled, a slow burning smile that crept first around the edges of his full lips and eventually ignited into a full-on grin as the *noes* increased. I played the innocente to the hilt. It was all Antonio could do not to murmur *¡Dorado!* under his breath. By this time I was sucking the dregs of the mojito out of the bottom of the glass, and, not wanting to drink too much of the questionable ice water that was rapidly amassing, I ordered another, casually asking him if he wanted anything.

He kind of pulled back in a machoesque move. "Una cerveza." Then, "Wan beer."

I signalled to the bartender. I knew my I've-got-money moves were starting to turn Antonio on.

"Where are joo staying?" he asked next.

I told him I had an Airbnb a few blocks away. He asked if it was nice. Was I happy with it? Then he launched into a description of an Airbnb a friend of his rented out. "Eet has a biew of the Malecón, it's bery spacious, aire conditioning, king-size bed. Joo would *looooooooove* it!"

I told him I had already paid in advance for my accommodation and couldn't now change it.

"Oh. I unnerstan. But maybe ... joo would like to see it anyways? It is bery nice. Maybe when joo come back nex tine? Or eef you have a fren who wants to come to Cuba?"

It crossed my mind at this point that the repertoire of jineter-
ismo had just been extended to touting Airbnbs. It used to be pala-
dares, and of course rum, cigars, mulattas, Santería. Now it was

- "a trip to the colonial with modern comfort"
- "7 minutes to the Capitolio, 6 minutes to the
  Malecón!"
- "local and authentic"
- "strategically located to enjoy the essence of the city
  in its most pure form!"

Wow. You coulda made a killing here. You could have plas-
tered every extrañera across every king-size bed "within walking
distance of the Prado." Qué lástima.

I toyed with the idea of going with Antonio to view the Airbnb.
I really did. But the thought of my sagging tetas pressed up against
his muscular chest was more than even I could stand. It wears
on you, it really does, the way that Cuban men can just make
love to you day and night with only their eyes, their words, those
damn winks. *Make love* in the old-fashioned sense, not take-off-
your-clothes-slap-on-a-condom sex with a stranger, but *seduction*.
If you're not careful, you can actually start to believe that they are
really smitten with you. I knew you were a master at this — it was
your treasure and your downfall.

Antonio was asking me for my phone number. I was getting
bored with the game now. This is the problem. I get bored easily;
I know too much. Waaaay more than any extrañera should know.
You taught me that. I can't even thank you for all that wisdom now
because, well, because you went away.

He suddenly noticed the book I had lying next to my handbag:
Los orishas en Cuba.

"Oh! Joo are innerrested in our religion?" He pointed to the idé
on his left wrist. "Look." He indicated. "Ellegua."

My interest in the game resumed. "Who is he?" I fauxed naïveté.

"He is … the dueño of the crossroads. He is my father." Antonio smiled broadly. Such beautiful teeth.

I threw gasoline on the fire. "I'd really like to know more about the religion. Do you know of any ceremonies I could go to? Are foreigners allowed?"

His eyes got wide. "¡Siiiiiiiiiiiiii!" He pulled out a cellphone and quickly pressed a few keys, then started shouting into the phone so the whole café could hear. "Victor. Es Toni. ¿A que hora es el cajón? Okay … okay … a las cuatro. Bárbaro. Dale … dale. Chao."

I'll tell you what happened next. Antonio took me to that cajón. He also took me to see the Airbnb on the way to the cajón, but I reeeeaaaaallyy don't want to tell you what happened up in there because, well, I was going to a ceremony for the dead. I had no business going unclean, but I got caught up in something, and playing the game, I couldn't let Antonio know that I knew about these things, sooooo I played the game along with him, him pretending to be smitten with me and me pretending like I didn't know what a damn cajón was, and after we were done I just splashed some Florida water on myself before we went into that cajón so that I wouldn't smell like a total puta and the muertos wouldn't call out my putería.

When we arrived, the drummers were hot as hell, and people were up and dancing. Somebody's Congo came down and tore up the place. I started feeling that familiar feeling, like I was slowly being anesthetized, my eyelids getting heavy, strange muscle twitches, running hot and cold, needing to dance to those drums. When the dude hit those maracas high — tshtshtshtshtshtshtshtsh — I trembled and nearly fell out. Someone came and steadied me. Antonio was nowhere to be found. A middle-aged woman wearing an Oyá skirt led me to a chair; someone else brought me a bottle of water (clearly they knew I was a foreigner). Where was Antonio, you ask? As I came out of my stupor I saw him across the room, eyes glazed, trembling like a chekeré itself. No one was helping him, and he started to stumble, damn near knocking over a small table. Then his glassy, bulging eyes focused on *me*, and he strode, big strides now, and stood in front of me, our knees touching.

"¡MI BANDERA!" he said, in a voice I thought sounded familiar. It hadn't yet registered.

"Oye," you said. "*¡Mi bandera roja!*"

I looked up into Antonio's eyes, only they weren't his eyes, they were *your* eyes, the same eyes I remembered that could morph from your medium brown into a tiger's-eye topaz, a transformation I couldn't understand then but which now made perfect sense. It was *your* voice calling for the red bandana.

"Yo no lo tengo," I told you. Ha ha, I wasn't going to give in so easily. Yes, I know you come from Havana, but *did you really have to follow me here?*

"Putaendo, as usual," you said. I couldn't even be embarrassed in front of all these people. If they only knew how much fucking around you had done in our time together.

"¿Qué tú quieres?" I was getting tired of the game again. You seriously came all the way across time and space to ask me for some damn red bandana?

Your eyes flashed black now. Like two black holes, like two cold cold ebony coals. Infinite. I felt the icy chill, this time through my entire body.

I realized I didn't quite know where I was. I had lost my head after the trip to the Airbnb and hadn't been paying attention when Antonio was directing the taxi driver to get us to the cajón. Now I wanted to get out of there — and fast.

"¿Te gusta mi caballo?" you asked. Do you like my horse? Then you laughed, hard, so hard I swore the walls shook. Or was it the drums? The drummers had not let up. I *really* needed to get out of there.

Who was I really fucking with? You? Antonio? Had you sent Antonio to me? For me? Did Antonio even belong to the land of the living?

¡Coñññññññño!

I got up off my chair and ran out of there. I know you followed me. You are still following me. Now I have to figure out how to get rid of you. It's 3:00 a.m. and I am up drinking cafecitos and smoking Populares to stay awake. I don't want to fall asleep, and see your face hovering above me, eyes switching from black to tiger's-eye topaz then back to black. ¡Déjame en paz! Leave me in peace! You know you got what you deserved, and if I have to carry you back into the cemetery a second time, I will.

"The Death of Caribana"

The host will admit you to the meeting shortly.

I don't even know why I came today. After all these years and all the headache and heartache, the backstabbings and the bobol, I really need to sit here and listen to some academic talk about how everything we built, all the blood, sweat, and tears, the late nights and long hours, the labours of love, how all that is just dead? Boy, ah too old for this.

> Thanks for coming everyone. I invited you here today because I wanted to introduce you to a script I am developing called "The Death of Caribana." I know you all have some vested interest in this great, amazing festival that

we, Caribbean people in Canada, created, which has persisted for over fifty years. I thought you would be good
people to talk to, and people from whom I can elicit feedback for my project.

*Violet looks tired. It's been a while since I've seen her, but damn,
this pandemic hasn't really been good to her. But then again, we all
probably look like shit right now. Still, woman could have made an
attempt and put on some goddamn makeup!*

In this film/memory, I am presenting the case that
Caribana as we knew it actually died a long time ago and
every August we are only resurrecting and excavating a
rotting corpse, rotting because it still has a presence —
a horrible stench and an unbearable unsightliness. The
process of putrefaction is not yet completed. So here we
are in this not-yet-complete phase, and I am asking the
people in the film, and the audience, what now?

*Okay, I'll bite. Because I don't like the stench of rotting corpse, I have
not attended Caribana in years!*

So I thought we could all go around and introduce ourselves. I'll start. I'm Violet McGinty, assistant professor in
Black diasporic studies at Darlington College, and the 2025
recipient of a Globalized Strategy Canadian Government
grant, as well as a Toronto Artistic Council Performative
Self grant. I am investigating the development and dis-
integration of Caribana/Toronto Caribbean Carnival/
WhatsApp Jump Up Festival. In particular I am interrogating the nuances within the interstices that are found within our Caribbean cultural milieu and juxtaposition within a
diasporic, transnational, and transgressive space. How we

have negotiated our melanated beings as cross-sectioned subjects transfixed, transposed, and transmogrified within the settler colonial gaze is of specific interest to me. Finally, I am seeking a robust closure regarding the ongoing and implicit cultural appropriation that is a vestige of both settler and exploitative colonial forms, vis-à-vis the White supremacist dialectical space, as well as within the more creolized, ambient, and audacious Anthropocene.

De actual fuck ...

Okay, so I will start off with the person at the top left of my screen — Miss Biggs?

GOOD DAY, HEVERYONE. I AM MISS BIGGS AND I HAM A COMMUNITY ACTIVIST AND SCHOLAR, ORIGINALLY FROM CLARENDON, JAMAICA. I HAVE WRITTEN A BOOK ON THE CARIBBEAN COMMUNITY IN CANADA ENTITLED *NUFF A GWAN: BLACK PEOPLE A RUN TINGS IN CANADA.* I AM ALSO PAST PRESIDENT OF THE JAMCAN NETWORK CENTRE AND THE PROFESSIONAL BLACK CANADIAN NETWORK. I HAVE BEEN A PARTICIPANT IN CARIBANA FOR OVER TIRTY YEARS, SO I TINK I HAVE A LOT TO SAY PON DE SUBJECT.

Thanks, Miss Biggs. Next I see ... Shira?

It's pronounced "Sheera."

My apologies. Shira, can you please introduce yourself?

Hello, everyone, hi, hi. My name is Shira Hospedales and I come from the loooovely twin island nation of

Trinidad and Tobago. I have been playing mahs for
as long as I can remembah and I come from a long
line of masqueradahs and Cahnival people. My uncle
migrated to Canada in 1967 and stahted one of the
fust Caribana bands, Wholigans. We were the fust
band to bring bikini and bead mas to Cahnada and I
myself have played Queen of the Band for Wholigans
for fourteen years, winning the title for nine of those
years. I am really happy to be heah today and I hope
I can make a meaningful contribution to Dr. Violet's
research!

Awright, so we have a CornVunt gyal up in de mix.

| Thanks, Shira. Next I see ... Belly Tapia?

Right, so my name is Betty Tapia and I was involved
for many years as both a participant and a contributor
to the production of Caribana. I have been less active
in recent years as, honestly, for me, the festival has lost
a lot of its meaning. So I hope we can generate some
discussion here about why that is and how we can perhaps revive it for the younger generations.

*Yuh lie, gyal, you dohn give a damn bout de next generation. They
could suck salt for all you care. Dese people had something so nice and
dey jus dash it wey as usual, and dis nex generation coming up dohn
know dey ass from dey elbow, and everyting is trans this and vegan
dat and pronouns and save the penguins from the meltin polar ice caps
and one setta shit. Dey don't even know what a good wine is, throwing
dey vagina dong on de dutty pavement and trying to be Cardi X and
Megan D Horse ... setta lorseness!*

Thanks so much, Betty. I am hoping for some great discussion, too! Next I see ... Riyad?

Hi, everyone. My name is Riyad Chanderband and I have been playing mas, making mas, eating mas, sleeping mas ... Ah, just kidding! I *love* Carnival and Caribana equally, and I make sure I attend both and play mehself to de fullest every year! I do hear what Betty is saying about Caribana having lost some of its meaning, but I also think this gives us the opportunity to make some important and significant changes to de festival and maybe transform some ole time traditions. I for one would like to see a greater LGBTQI2S+ presence at Caribana. I mean, a lot of us have been going for years, but we have remained on the fringes, in the shadows, and I think it is time for that to stop. We have *never* really fit into Pride and we all know why that is, so it's time we claimed our rightful place at Caribana!

Riyad, I am so glad you said that because I could not agree with you more!

Thanks, Shira! Hope to see you on the road next month. Yuh buy yuh ticket as yet, gyal?

Yes man, long time!

All right, Riyad and Shira, you two, let's not rub it in too much for those of us who can't make it to Carnival this year. That would be me!

Cheeeupsss, well, why is dat Violet? Yuh head too far inside yuh book! What bacchanal is this now een de chat?

Riyad Chanderband: Shira gyal ah havin a pre-Carnival lime by me. Bring yuh man an come!

Shira Hospedales: Alright but no man ... is woman ah bringing!

Riyad Chanderband: What?! Gyal wha'appen, yuh switch sides?

Shira Hospedales: No I am an equal opportunity employer. Ah want to taste the rainbow LOL!

Riyad Chanderband: Gyal yuh too rude!

Okay, well, thanks, everyone, for these introductions, and now I would like to start the conversation going with my first question: What does Caribana mean to you? Who would like to start? Miss Biggs, I see your hand up.

FOR ME, CARIBANA HAS BEEN THE ONLY TRUE REP-RESENTATION OF BLACK AND AFRO-CARIBBEAN CUL-TURE THAT WE HAVE HAD HERE AS BLACK PEOPLE IN CANADA AND IT IS *FOR US* AND *BY US*. IT IS WHOLLY OUR OWN AND NOBODY CAN'T TOUCH IT OR TAKE IT WAY FROM US, ALDOUGH MANY HAVE TRIED. EVERYWHERE BLACK PEOPLE GO WE LEAVE OUR MARK — NEW YORK HAS ITS LABOR DAY PARADE AND MIAMI HAVE ITS CARNIVAL AND ENGLAND HAVE ITS BRIXTON CARNIVAL ...

Wait, did she jus say Brixton Carnival? Since when Brixton have a Carnival? Uhhhh, who is going to be the one to tell her? Laaawd,

*de woman come heah like she some kinda Carnival hexpert but she
dohn even know the name of the big big Carnival that been running
in England for over fifty years?* She dohn even know is Notting Hill
Carnival self? *Cheeeupsss!*
     *An why is she talking about Black? It is more than just Blackness.
Alla allwe movin to de same riddim. Indians gettin on Chiney gettin
on even dem French Creole an dem really winin dong low. Never
mind all de mixup mixup people! Caribana was one of the only times
in this country I really saw home, home all around me. Not just this
Black face representation — we not like Jamaica, yuh know! Nor
Barbados! Cheups! Lawd, dese people.*
     Looks like Riyad gonna jump een de fray.

Okay, so I just want to say here that we need to remember
that Caribbean communities are *diverse* and Caribana was
not, nor has ever been, a solely *Black* festival, and even
that term is problematic because it really screams *African
American*, which is not who we are, is it? I mean, the last
time I checked, it is a whole lot of people of different races
and ethnic backgrounds who both produce and participate in
Caribana, not just people of African descent —

AH TRUE. TANK YOU, MEH COOLIE BREDREN, FOR
POINTING THAT OUT —

Uh yeah, and that *coolie* word? *Not* okay, okay? Like, it's the
equivalent of the N-word for us, so, like, no, um, okay?

WELL, ME NO KNOW DAT. WE USE DAT WORD IN
JAMAICA HAWL DE TIME. IS EVEN LIKE A COMPLI-
MENT AN TING, LIKE IF YOU SAY "SHE HAD NICE COO-
LIE HAIR" AN TING.

Ohhhh-ouiiii lawd, Miss Biggs done step in it now! Watch Violet de professor gonna school she.

> And these are some of the tensions we need to unpack,
> aren't they? The intra-community issues that have kept
> us divided and apart all these years. I guess I should inter-
> ject to remind everyone here to be respectful of our dif-
> ferences and ensure that any language or terms you are
> using are non-offensive to those present here, and even
> beyond the confines of this Zoom room, okay? Let's try to
> keep this a safe space.

*Hmmm, well, Biggsy gonna hafta boil dong like bhaji now. It good.
The million of times I get een an argument with someone from Jamaica
who want to insist that Carnival is a Jamaican thing, dat is dey who
bring it here, dat Jamaicans know all about what a Carnival is. And
den I have to politely point out to dem dat, no, it is not and never
was a Jamaican tradition, dat it was actually imported into Jamaica
by bandleader Byron Lee in the 1980s as a middle-class, brown-
skin, uptown ting, and dat dere is no lengthy history nor tradition
of Carnival anyting in dat country because the British dominated
dere for hundreds of years and we all know the dour British were not
Carnival people!*
Oh wait, Shere Khan ha someting to say!

> I just think we need to remembah that the *spirit* of
> Cahnival really comes out of the Trinidadian all-o'-
> we-is-one melting pot callaloo that so many of us
> come from, and that we know and love. It is in our
> blood and in our bones — as calypsonian David
> Rudder sang, "Trini to de bone." So that is *really* what
> Caribana means to me and always has, and for my
> parents, too — even my grandparents before them!

They were jumping up in Port-of-Spain back in the
1950s!

Well, yes, she representin for de callaloo and dem, all de nowhereians.

| Miss Biggs, I see your hand?

YES, I JUST WANTED TO RESPOND TO SHIRA COM-
MENT. I HAM A JAMAICAN AND I KNOW LOTS OF
JAMAICANS WHO CONTRIBUTE TO CARIBANA, WHO
PLAY DERE MAS AND SUPPORT DE FESTIVAL, AND
EVEN OUTSIDE OF JAMAICANS THERE ARE OTHER
CARIBBEAN PEOPLE WHO ATTEND CARIBANA AND
PARTICIPATE IN CARIBANA LIKE GRENADIANS AND
BAJANS AND EVEN DE GUYANESE DEM, SO I TAKE OF-
FENCE TO THAT STATEMENT THAT THIS IS REALLY A
TRINIDADIAN FESTIVAL —

Okay, I didn't say Caribana was a Trinidadian festival.
I said for *me* —

RIGHT, GOOD, BUT YOU HAFFI MEMBER. YOU HAFFI
MEMBER DAT DERE ARE MANY MORE JAMAICANS UP
HERE IN CANADA THAN TRINIDADIANS, SO YOU CAN-
NOT JUST DOMINATE EVERYTING JUST SO. YOU HAFFI
LEAVE ROOM FOR UDDER PEOPLE.

Ah wonder if Shere Khan gonna even bodda respond to dis cunumunu.

So, I'd just like to interject here and mention that we
have had tensions about authenticity and ownership of
this festival since sometime in the 1990s. Some of you
may recall the time these tensions really boiled over and

we had a "hostage" situation, a year where a number of
Jamaican participants felt they had been treated unfairly
by the Festival Management Committee, and they even
attempted to stop the parade of bands.

*I remember dis very clearly because I was dere! Vex like hell, we only
standin up ready to get on de road an dese setta Jamaican jackass-
es really tryin to bring violence to de parade. Violence, yuh hear?
Cheups. Want to treaten to beat up masqueraders an ting!*

So, let's move on. The next question I would like to bring to
the group is, what legacy if any do you think Caribana has
brought to the next generation of Caribbean Canadians?
Many of us grew up in families where Caribana was a part
of our lives in one way or another. Do you think an appreciation for Caribana has been passed down through the
generations?

*What do dese people really know bout family and Caribana? Hmmph.
Dat is someting ah could really talk bout, oui, We breastfed our babies
at Caribana. Changed diapers at Caribana. Pushed toddlers een
strollers, played mas with our little ones. We were pregnant an still
chippin dong de road wit a big belly. Den dong to — we even push
our elders een wheelchairs at Caribana!*

*Cheups! An is vex it get me vex seein what has happened to dis
so-called Carnival tradition up here. Allyuh didn't raise yuh chirren
right! Allyuh raise one setta hooligans, especially dem who ent have
no Carnival tradition een dey blood an bone, allyuh who only feel
is a free-for-all. Shere Khan have a point, oui! Yuh didn't teach yuh
chirren nuttin bout broughtupcy and manners! I will never forget one
Caribana, ah chippin dong de road like normal, likin mehself, when
ah see granny next to me chippin, going dong de road too, silver plaits
een she head, she wrinkled tot tots cradled een a bikini top, and she*

movin proud and dignified, a proud African woman playin she little mas! An was to see dis posse ah stinkin rank yutes, dey was mashin up de people pretty mas, breaking up all de wire bendin and decoration, and den one a dem push granny dong on de pavement face fus! Ah see blood, oui! Is fight ah wanted to fight dem stink yutes, but dey done gone orf tru de crowd fas fas. All ah could do was assist granny and help she up, me and some udder masqueraders. Such a sad day. A sad day, ah tell yuh.

And that was not the only setta violation and bad behaviour ah did see on de road — a nex time wasn't even we people! Dem American an dem, a setta Yankee frat boys, wit big ugly keloid brandin scars on dey biceps, like dey was still een slavery times, claimed by some slave master! Ah remember clear as day, seein a group a dem huntin tru de crowd one Caribana. Dey was hunting fuh young gyal! Was about de time dat dem small video camera an dem come out, before everybody had a camera on dey phone, and dese setta wicked yutes was huntin gyal to grab up and grope up and hump up right dey, videotaping like dey was makin some kinda porn right een de people public road! What kinda jackass behaviour is dat?

Ai, here come Shere Khan again.

Well, I, along with a numbah of bandleadahs, have started this initiative where we go into the schools, pahticulahly in hot-spot areas —

Did she really now say "hot-spot areas"? Woman, dis not Trinidad! We dohn have hot-spot here. We have "priority neighbourhoods"! Lawdamercy.

— and we are trying to teach the children about mah-hhs, what is the history of mahhhs, why mahhhs is so important for Cahribbean people, and how much fun it is, and then we encoourage them to make they-ah

own costume. We hold a little workshop where we
teach them some basics about mahhhs design and
so on. So I don't know if that answers your question
or not —

No, it does not, CornVunt gyal.

— but I see that as one way that we cahn keep the
tradition alive by ensuring that future generations
cahn know about these traditions and keep them
alive!

| Thanks, Shira. Riyad, I see you have your hand up?

Yes, ah just had a question for Shira. These kids that you
are teaching these traditions to, are they all Caribbean kids?

No, they come from a variety of cultural backgrounds.
They come from everywhere in the world. You know,
Toronto. Multicultural.

Okay, so ... don't you think that might be problematic in that
some of these kids might take our culture and appropriate it
and then try to market our culture back to us? I mean, I am
just wondering if we shouldn't be more careful about who we
teach these important cultural legacies to.

Well, I hahve to disagree with you, Riyad. I think our
culture is so be-yoo-tee-ful and so rich that we really
should share it with the world! You know what they
say — we Trinis are the happiest people on Earth! And
I believe that! God really is a Trini!

HEXCUSE MEH BUT EAR WE GO AGAIN WIT DE FOCUS ON TRINIS! MEMBER IS NOT TRINIS ALONE EAR AT CARIBANA! NO SUH!

Sorry, Miss Diggs, but you know we have to give credit where credit is due, and you do know it was us Trinis who brought Caribana here to begin with, so —

IS MISS BIGGS, MA'AM. MISS *BIGGS*!

Lawd, here dey go again. Jamaica and Trinidad still fightin ever since Federation fell apart in 1959, but, really and truly, Shere Khan have a point — again. Ah mean, ah cyan unnerstan why it is Jamaicans feel it is dey mus claim everyting! We dohn try an claim dey reggae music, nor dey dancehall (well dey could keep dat wholesale), neither dey jerk chicken nor dey pattie and all dem ting dey does eat. We dohn try to claim Rasta nor Bob Marley. All yuh ent have enough to be proud of? Yuh mus try and put de stamp uh JAMAICA on everything? Cheups!

But Riyad mekkin a good point, too, and if these two would just hush, I mighta jump up an defend him. Because, no lie, ah seein all kinda Becky and Karen dese days tryna get een de mas business, ah see dey want to open up mas camp and lead section and design King and Queen of de Band costume an all kinda mad ting, down to dey tryna learn, ah mean steal, de art of wirebending, a real precious art form we have dat come from we. And because we own pickney and dem ent even caring bout dey legacy, jus now de whole a Caribana gonna be one setta Becky and Karen traipsing down de Lakeshore wit dey Victoria's Secret angel wings and one setta Coachella feather and me ent know what. What de assss dey know bout resistance? What dey know about colonialism, slavery, indentureship, de plantation? Is to get me vex, oui! What dey feel it is, some kinda Halloween in August? An one setta dotishness wit dem — ah see one Miss Becky online tryna sell she used mas costume, ah mean used, all stink up, sweat up, poom poom sweat-dong drawers and she sweat-up bra top, and is sell she tryna sell online as if is some Halloween costume she wear to some house party, or some "vintage" couture! Woman! Dat panty yuh had on was quite up een yuh crotch an cacahole drinkin een yuh sweat and fluids fuh a whooooole day a chippin and winin and jumpin dong de Lakeshore een de summer sun — yuh mad uh wha? Who de asss want dat frowsiness now? Cheups! An she was chargin big big money fuh eet! *Ah done talk!*

Seem like dey still arguin about Trinidad versus Jamaica and now Violet hadda trow she hat in de ring tryna ease de tension, talkin bout how she fadder from Barbados and she half Bajan and Bajans does real wuk up. Ting is, I remember how we raised our kids to appreciate mas and Caribana, how we go out we way to ensure dey knew dey culture, teaching them how to wine, how to jump and wave, but you feel dey now comin to Caribana? Half a dem cyan be bothered! Some of them sayin that is too frivolous for them, but dey well ready to jump out to defend Indigenous land rights, and to speak out about anti-Black racism and police brutality, this whole Black Lives Matter ting! Jeezanages, they only lookin to America to tell them what to do, what to wear, how to speak, how to be "Black" — well, ah too sorry, but last time I checked it have a whooooole heap a people who does call themselves Black or who get called Black and not one ah dem is de damn same. All a we "Black" people just people same way so — some are chupidee, some feel dey bright, and some come from de devil heself!

Look like Violet callin a time out.

All right, well, I want to bring us back on track, as I am conscious of the time. This next question, I really want us all to dig deep and be big people here. We are all big people. Very often we in the Caribbean Canadian community are quick to lay blame for the failures and pitfalls of Caribana. We blame the government, we blame the police, we blame systemic racism, we blame White Canadians. *I am taking responsibility and I feel it is something all of we who are of Caribbean descent and who have participated in Caribana and who have claimed Caribana as our own — we have to admit that we dropped the ball. We* have no one to blame but ourselves. *We* have to admit there is a problem — a problem in our communities, in our families, in ourselves. So, my question to you is, where have we as Caribbean people failed Caribana? Riyad?

Okay, well, first of all I want to say that there *is* such a thing as systemic racism, so I don't think we should just discount that, and I don't think it is really fair to put all the blame, all the onus on *us*. That is a blame-the-victim mentality. So I'm not sure I am okay with the framing of this question —

I HADDA AGREE WITH MY INDIAN BREDREN HERE. BLACK PEOPLE HAVE BEEN HELD DOWN AND BEAT DOWN BY DE STATE AND DE POLICE AN TING FOR TOO TOO LONG AND THIS IS SOMETHING I TALK ABOUT IN MY BOOK, ABOUT HOW WE AS BLACK PEOPLE NEED TO RISE UP IN THE SPIRIT OF MARCUS MOSIAH GARVEY AND BOB MARLEY AND FREE OURSELVES FROM MENTAL SLAVERY!

She including Riyad een she "Black people"? 'Cause I am very confused right now.

Dr. Violet, I also have to agree with what has just been said. As I stated, my family has been involved in the production of mahhhs and the promotion of Cahribana and we have gone into the poor downtrodden communities in Toronto and really worked

with these children and brought the joy of Cahnival
and Cahribana and mahhhhs to them, so I don't know
that I or my family can say that we have not done
our part. So I don't know if it is really fair to blame
us Caribbean people as if to say we have not done
enough! Cahnival and Cahribana are such wonderful
traditions, of course other people are going to want
to get involved and have all the fun they see us having! So it is inevitable that this festival would change
over time, and that other people, not just Caribbean
people, would get involved! I think that is a *good*
thing. I mean, imitation is the sincerest form of flat-
tery, isn't that so? I feel *proud* when I see someone
who is not from the Caribbean wearing a mahhhs
costume and chipping down the road at Caribana,
waving a *Canadian* flag! As a Trinidadian I feel proud!

| Betty? What are your thoughts on this?

*Oh ho, so Violet want to put me on de spot? Well ah hope is ready dey
ready fuh what I had to say.*

Look, Violet ent wrong. At some point we hadta be
"big people," as she say, and face facts. This is one of
the biggest problems we as a people have. And when I
say "we as a people," I want to make it clear I am not
only speaking about Black people. Because whatever
Caribana is it ent just Black, never was. Same with
Carnival. Its roots are African *and* European, and
then everybody and everything that came afterward.

And this is the problem. We never really *see* ourselves.
We always seeing ourselves through someone else's

eyes. Imagining ourselves through someone else's im-
agination. The colonizer told us who we were, and if
we didn't agree, we were whipped, punished, raped,
even killed! We passed on that madness to our kids.
Always trying to please somebody else. Always believing when somebody else try and come and tell us who
we are, where we come from. But We is We. If you
know your history — even some of it — that is a start.
But our kids don't know our history. Either we never
learned it, or we were too ashamed to pass it on to our
kids. So they looking everywhere for meaning. They
looking to Beyoncé and Cardi B and Jay-Z and Drake.
Dey think dey history is Martin and Malcolm. Dey
looking south of the border, not past the USA entirely
and into the Caribbean. And those that know they
are from the Caribbean, that usually means they only
know about their tiny corner of it: Jamaica, Trinidad,
Guyana, Barbados. But we all here now — we have
all been thrown together just like they did to us on
the plantation, so we needed to figure out a way to
unify and build strength in that. We were supposed
to have done that from the beginning of us coming to
this country. We missed that opportunity. Unless you
fully understand that, that we have our own unique
histories and identities, and that we are *complex*, once
you know and embrace that, then no matter how long
you have lived up here, or even if you were born up
here but you still know good and well where you come
from, you cannot be sidetracked. You cannot lose what
is precious and special and important to that sense of
self. But we did lose that. We were lax. We wasted
time bickering amongst ourselves instead of uniting;
we failed our kids, and America took over. We lost our

heritage, we gave it away, we opposed each other. We forgot to include our children in the running of this thing called Caribana. And so here we are.

| Thanks so much for that, Betty.

Well, ah done talk. What more is there to tell dem? Ting is, for me this ting wrap up an bury long time. Once upon a time, there was a magic to de whole event leading up to de Big Saturday. We didn't have Jouvert, no, but ah could tell yuh bout biking dong University Avenue early early Saturday morning, watchin all de police barriers settin up, awaitin de crowds, de place still an clean, a big miles-long stage waiting for all de warmth an love an joy an colour to descend. It had magic een dat air. Ah used to fly dong University Avenue on meh bicycle, blessin de space, de slope of de street carryin meh so ah didn't even have to peddle, imaginin de tousands of feet dat would be chippin chippin chippin, carryin us dong to de lake. Dere was a natural flow to dat route, dong hill to a lake. It ent had dat now. Now dey had people chippin alongside a lake to ... what? A sign sayin TURN MUSIC OFF NOW, *held by a minion of Babylon wit a gun an badge? Right dey dey kill de ting. Movin it from its fus sacred space, dat was de fus nail een de coffin, an it never recover. Den dey change up de name — yuh cyan change up a name! Yuh cyan tek de vibration of someting dat was spoken een reverence, een love, een awe, een bliss, een excitement, by millions of people. A name has a vibration to it! Instead dey stink it up by not only changin de name but addin a corporate label to it! Yuh mad uh wha? Second nail in de coffin, bwoy!*

An de tird and fourt nails? We own greediness and we own stubbornness! It always have some smart man ready to run wit de money, it always have some bobol runnin behind the scenes, it always have some jackass cookin de books and ruinin eet fuh everybody else. Wedder we learn dat behaviour wholesale from de colonizer or what, or wedder dat was part of de toolkit of our survival from long time, me ent

*care. Dat was de tird nail, and the fourt was stubbornly and stingily
holding on to de ting as if eet was only for people who migrated from
Trinidad in de 1960s and 1970s, makin fun ah we chirren who was
born up heah, who didn't always know de right creole word to use,
or understand de lyrics to a calypso, or how to cook a real pelau or a
good curry. We made fun ah dem an didn't bodda to pass on de beauty
of dis ting. We called dem Canadians and den chastised dem for not
wanting to carry de torch of dere own legacy! Too chupid! Violet damn
right — no one to blame but weselves!*

I want to thank everyone today for your participation and
I will keep you all posted as to how things progress with
the project. Before we close, I would like to ask each of
you if you have any final words.

*Ashes to ashes, dust to dust ... inna lillahi wa inna ilayhi raji'un ...
Ibae bae tonu ... aatma ko sadgati prapt ho. Last rites.*

IT MAKES ME VERY SAD TO HEAR ALL THE DIVISION
GOING ON WITH US AROUND THIS FESTIVAL. WE
NEED MORE LOVE AND UNITY, PEOPLE! I WANT TO
BE ABLE TO BRING MY GRANDPICKNEY AND GREAT
GRANDPICKNEY TO CARIBANA. WHAT I ENVISION FOR
THIS FESTIVAL IS THAT WE CAN EXPAND IT, WE CAN
INCLUDE MORE PEOPLE TO PARTICIPATE, WE HAVE
LOTS OF OUR AFRICAN BROTHERS AND SISTERS WHO
ARE NOW COMING HERE, OUR PEOPLE FROM NIGERIA
AND GHANA AND SOMALIA AND OTHER PARTS OF
THE MOTHERLAND. WE SHOULD COME TOGETHER
AND MAKE THIS A PAN-AFRICAN FESTIVAL AND THAT
WAY WE CAN ENSURE THAT OUR CULTURE IS NOT
LOST. ANOTHER GROUP THAT HAS BEEN LEFT OUT IS
THE RASTA. WHY WE DON'T HAVE A RASTA FLOAT, A
RASTA MUSIC TRUCK? SO, I AM PUTTING THESE IDEAS

FORWARD AS A WAY WE COULD REVIVE CARIBANA
AND HAVE SOMETHING TO PASS ONTO THE NEXT
GENERATIONS.

| Thanks, Miss Biggs. Shira?

I think I already stated this, but I feel it's time that
Caribana become a truly multicultural festival. There
are even other people who have Cahnival traditions
that are not included in the parade — like Brazilians,
Cubans, Dominicans, Colombians. I, too, want to be
able to bring my children to Caribana one day! And
yes, as Miss Biggs said, we need to focus on *unity*.
Not just unity of races but of *people*. Going back
to what Riyad said earlier, there are a lot of people
right here in Toronto who feel unwelcome and shut
out of Caribana and that should *not* be the case. So,
greater inclusion, greater acceptance, more love, less
division!

| Thank you, Shira. Riyad?

I am going to echo what Shira just said, and what I already
mentioned. When you go to Trinidad's Carnival, you see a
strong presence of gay and lesbian and other people on
the road, playing mas, in the fêtes. This has become com-
monplace. But you just don't see that at Caribana, which is
nonsensical since we have one of the largest populations
of LGBTQI2S+ people in North America, if not the world!
Toronto is *known* as a place of acceptance of diversity, but
we have yet to diversify Caribana, so for me *that* is what
really needs to happen going forward!

| Thank you, Riyad. Anyone else?

No, ah done talk. Ah have me memories. I remember de great glory of the Kings and Queens tailgate party behind Lamport Stadium — well, we call eet a lime, and dis one happened to be a car lime. Ready-made bar pop out de trunk, speaker system blasting, lil fold-out chairs for moms and pops to recline wit de drink holder. Like half a Brooklyn descend one year — pimped-out cars and saga boys and girls, and everybody hailing everybody else: "Come tek a drink nah, man!" "Boysie lehwe fyah one!" De show behind de show. A stone's trow from dere, Afropan panyard een full swing. Was a time to fuhget you was een Canada. Pan beatin sweet, people limin, DJ spinnin, drinks flowin. Was niceness self. And Caribana Saturday, de edgy excitement as you get up early to put on yuh makeup. Yuh nails already on point, and yuh shoes done spray paint an glitter up, and now was to trow glitter on yuhself an each an everybody who passed by 'cause you always by someone or dey by you havin de warm-up lime. And den was to go dong to Exhibition Place, some a de brave ones tekkin TTC, de rest of us een cars or cabs, and den to step out an see all a we een we beauty an extravagance — mama! Fillin up Exhibition Grounds, tourists jockeying to take a pic wit yuh, yuh feel is real paparazzi! An dose unforgettable hours on de road, de sheer joy of chippin and winin and grindin and sippin and trowin waist and display. An all de little gems you would look for every year — de Grenadian posse on de road een dey jab jab costumes, glitterin mirrors an rags, trowing powder like nobody business, and wavin dey bush high een de air. Somebody playin a ole mas een de road, a devil, a gorilla, a Dame Lorraine, holding up a sign een Trinbagonian to make dere political statement een de middle of bikinis and beads. And de endless an joyful bouncin up of long-lost friends and family, hearin someone bawl yuh name from behine de police barriers, or someone grabbin you up an jammin yuh on de road because dey recognize yuh bumper, lawwwwwwd!! An when it all done an yuh reach de sour face police holding up dey TURN MUSIC OFF NOW *sign, was to tun round quick quick and jump back up de road, to fine a nex band to jump wit til de end of de road, an again, an again! Was also to ride out before it got too dark, before too many waste yutes descended on de place an started dere roughness. An when yuh got home was to soak yuh foot een some Epsom salts because yuh couldn't believe de presshah dey had just undergone, had no idea yuh coulda dance for so long and nevah nevah nevah get tiyad.*

Was rell vibes back een de day. But jus like Trinidad Carnival, dat too change an transform an become someting else, someting that lost its way. But maybe that is just de way eet is. Noting lass forever. Everyting hadta change. Ah ole now, ah had my times. Who knows? Dey might just surprise us.

| Betty?

    Ah good.

| All right then, I want to thank everyone again for your participation, and I will be in touch as things progress. Take care everyone and we'll talk soon!

Leave.

Ah done lef long time.

Suite as Sugar

i. The sweetness of lies

The arkatia had promised them so much. It was such a long time ago that Old Ma and Old Pa, canecutters at Brechin Castle Estate in Caroni, could not even remember all the lies he had lied to them. When they arrived in Trinidad, they were sent to the plantation and the hard hard work began. The swinging, slashing, and chopping, hot sun, rain, blisters on hands, swinging slashing chopping, dust choking, muscles aching, your wielding arm feeling like it would come out its socket, the cutlass feeling like it was now a part of your anatomy, slashing chopping cutting. Then the beatings, the threats. A wooden, rotting row dwelling with no privacy and no air (they later learned the Creole people had lived there before them, under slavery), the soot and smoke of cooking fires, an overseer's eyes passing over Ma's backside too too much, and Pa looking to kill. And the cane, the endless cane that went on for miles, undulating in the breeze, then at once mocking you on the tepid breezeless days of the dry season, days that burned into your skin and your eyes and made you feel to dead. During the rainy season the canes hid all kinds of dangers — hookworms, snakes, scorpions, even the tiny day mosquitos that were relentless. At first, Ma had wondered how long they would have to stay in this place, if there was any way out of this indentureship contract they had unwittingly put their thumbprints to, if they would really be able to get back on a ship and return to India, rich and whole, ready for a better life (as the arkatia had intimated), after this nightmare was over. But now, as she looked out at the dark, vast sea of cane, black now, silhouetted by the pale blue and marine twilight sky, the majestic silver clouds, after a long day of being swallowed up in those same fields, and after sharing out the modest evening meal for Pa and herself, Ma knew they would never cross that kala pani, that black sea, again. They were here now. They had to make a life of it.

Long before Old Ma and Old Pa and thousands of others like them arrived in Trinidad, a French Creole named St. Hilaire Begorrat brought the succulent, fortuitous yellow sugar cane to the isle and set himself up as lord amongst his African slaves. For kicks he would hold court in a limestone cave overlooking the Diego Martin Valley, and like a pharaoh, insist they compose kaisos bragging about what a demon he was, what a terror, an evil satanic entity. His slaves knew this to be true, knew that for any insurrection they could be tortured or even killed in these same caves, hot red blood splashing on white walls, an indelible stain. Begorrat promised them freedom if they sang his praises; he promised he would leave something for them after he died — land, a ring, gold coins. The same people who hewed the forests of Diego Martin, who uprooted rocks and stumps, who broke up hard land to make it cultivatable, who planted the sweet sweet cane to enrich Begorrat, in the end were freed by the Slave Emancipation Act, and not by any crazed French Creole. So, as free human beings, they left his sugar plantation, knowing there was no sweetness in the lie; there was nothing to be had there, not with that Beelzebub and his megalomania.

Begorrat's former slaves were not alone. All over Trinidad, all over the English-speaking Caribbean, newly freed peoples were vacating the plantations, moving off into hills and valleys, anywhere they could start a new life away from the horrors of the whip, the rape, the torture, the insanity, and the endless lies. The planters, desperate to maintain their lavish lifestyles and the twisted hold they had on those considered subhuman, begged the Colonial Office in London to recruit Indians as replacement slaves. But the Colonial Office said no, no, we can no longer enslave people; it is now considered abhorrent. However, they suggested, let us find another way. They resurrected the system of indentureship (which had served them well before African enslavement), but this time, instead of their own starving British peasants, it was to be "coolies," dusty and emaciated, travelling by the hundreds, by the thousands, to the depot in Calcutta to listen to the arkatia spin lies, sweet lies, lies that could almost fill a hollow stomach they were so tempting, lies to swallow and stave off hunger that had become indelible. "Put your thumb here"; the arkatia indicated where on a piece of parchment. They then boarded the ships.

That first lie, spoken back in the mother country, was sweet because it promised escape from poverty, from death, from famine. The second lie, that the work was easy — that one was harder to swallow. Yes, there was food, there were rations, there was some meagre pay that got swallowed up by the elephant of the company store on the estate, which, through the mechanism of credit, kept one in perpetual debt. And this debt was compounded by additional debts, endless debts that kept piling up due to any infraction — insubordination, being caught off the plantation without a pass, deception. The work was crushing, back-breaking, limb burning, relentless, merciless. The third lie: that you could really go back home one day, see your village again, your maai, baboo, didi, bhai — but instead this green-and-yellow monster had you chained. Day in, day out, sun up, sun down, rain, cloud, wind, hoe, dig, plant, manure, weed, cut, burn, crush, boil, heave, tote, carry, fling, suck. Amidst this bitterness, you *could* consume sweetness every day, suck the cane you had cultivated, the cane that kept you subjugated. Sometimes that cane was all you had to consume. You buried your children in the canefield: this one died from malaria, that one from dysentery, a next one from malnutrition. The sweet smell of rotting flesh mixed with the smell of ripe cane. You believed the lie that said only five years, then return passage. You asked to go back. They said, "Another five years." You lied to yourself, saying, "It is my dharma."

ii. The sweetness of nectar

Doree came with her jahaji bundle, following her husband Boyo to Town, away from the canefields and the coolies, but she ended up in Coolie Town instead (its colonial name St. James), a haphazard ramshackle suburb, on Town's outskirts. The day they left, the heavy beras she wore clanged as she and Boyo made their way down the muddy track to Carapichaima, where they waited at the junction for a donkey cart. It was only when she saw the electric lights of Port-of-Spain ("Town" to the residents of the island) that Doree put on her leather slippers. She was excited and scared at the same time, and proud of Boyo, who had the courage to pick them up out of the canefield and bring her to this metropolis. Boyo had been visiting Town for a few months now, and had put things in place for her arrival. He carried her to a small board house on Lucknow Street, on the very edge of Coolie Town, and showed her the basic furniture he had managed to collect — a bed, a table and two chairs, a small rug. She soon set about establishing a kitchen garden and planting some trees, mango, tamarind, coconut, and lime.

Time passed in the little house, and she gave birth to three children in quick succession. With each child it seemed that Boyo changed more and more. He took up drinking, then going out nights with other men from the area. One night he came home smelling of some sweet perfume mixed with the scent of rum, and Doree felt so hurt and so ashamed she simply covered her face with her orhni and sat on the bed, looking at her hands. Boyo, drunk, fell asleep in a chair in the sitting room. He had taken to gambling on the main road. There were so many distractions in this place; it frightened Doree and she missed the only home she had ever known, the small village bordering the estate in the centre of the island. The allure of Town was apparently too much for Boyo (or perhaps it was the never-ending poverty, his children going to bed hungry night after night), because one day he simply disappeared. Doree tried asking some of the fellas she had seen him with if they knew where he was, but they shook their heads; one gave her a pitying look. Amongst them, a brash young fella with Hollywood features simply let her know that when she was ready for the next man, he would come calling. He even winked at her. She could not believe these Town people, these Town ways.

After a few months of first waiting hopefully for Boyo to return, and then grieving his loss, she grew tired of the neighbours feeling sorry for her, giving her a little flour, a little rice, some oil, some eggs. She realized that although she had come here to make a life with Boyo, if he had left her, there was nothing she could do except go to work. She started to make Indian delicacies: savoury pholourie with tamarind chutney, kurma, and barfi, and then a Creole woman down the road taught her how to make sugar cake and toolum, the round black balls of grated coconut and molasses. She sold from the front yard of the board house. Sometimes, in desperation, she would leave her children home or take the youngest one with her and sell out on the main road. She started to change the way she dressed: wanting to fit in more with Town, she had a seamstress sew her a few simple dresses. The orhni was folded up and put away. Another one of her kind neighbours gave her a pair of shoes she no longer wanted. Doree realized she could attract more customers if she looked more modern, more Town, if she smiled, if she exchanged some pleasantries with the people who came to buy. When her eldest son was old enough, he began to tend cows and hunt for shrimps and crabs along the shore. Those first months were hard, and some days all she and her children had to eat were the mangoes from the tree in the yard and some bhaji boiled in coconut milk. But Doree and her little family continued to struggle, and around the anniversary of Boyo's disappearance, the young brash man who had been so forward with Doree suddenly reappeared.

His name was David (it was really Davindra, but he said that was old-time thing and he was a Town man). He asked her if she wanted to go to the pictures. Doree had never seen the inside of a cinema; she had passed the Rialto so many times and had envied the people going in and out. She was shy with David, but still curious. The thought of going to the pictures was exciting. It seemed all she did was work and look after her children, and she was only nineteen. The truth was she was angry that Boyo had simply left her, when they had taken vows, been married under the bamboo. Didn't he care about karma? This David was so much better looking than her Boyo. She suddenly remembered how Boyo had come home smelling of perfume that night, and she looked David straight in his eye and agreed to a matinee date the next afternoon.

David knew Doree looked a bit out of place at the cinema with her simple dress and second-hand shoes, but what he saw was a diamond in the rough. He knew these country coolie girls were easy prey, especially ones like Doree who had been abandoned by their faithless husbands and had children to mind and no help. He had seen this scenario many times. He had also heard that Boyo was living with some Creole girl down in Carenage, like that woman saltfish had his head so tie up he had forgotten all about his wife and family.

Halfway through the picture David tried to take Doree's hand. She pulled away, unsure. No other man except Boyo had ever touched her. Next David tried to rest his hand on her knee. She pushed it off, firmly but gently. This dance continued through the second half of the movie. David, saying nothing, kept up his manoeuvres. Doree's heart was pounding, but the rest of her body was craving human contact, a man's touch. She was unsure. She felt it was wrong somehow for David to touch her, and yet she wanted him to sweep her off her feet the way that Paul Henreid was sweeping Bette Davis off her feet in the picture. So much had happened, so much had gone wrong. She realized too late a tear was falling from her eye. She moved to wipe it away.

David jumped at the opportunity. "You need a handkerchief? The story so sad?" He pulled a clean handkerchief from his pocket and gently dabbed her eyes.

The tenderness of that action overwhelmed Doree, and she stifled a sob. David wrapped his arm around her and gently coaxed her head down on his shoulder. He gave her the handkerchief to hold and rubbed her arm, comforting her.

They stayed like this for a few minutes, and then David said, "Hold on, I have something to make you feel better," and pulled a silver flask from his jacket pocket. He encouraged Doree to sip the rum slowly.

At first she thought she would choke, but after it went down and warmed her tummy, she found herself relaxing. She began to relax so much that when David next put his hand on her leg, she didn't object. When he turned her face toward him to kiss her ever so gently on the lips, she didn't flinch. In fact, she kissed him back. The music soared on the screen. It had been so long. He gave her another sip of the rum. She liked how she was beginning to feel. It was a way she had never felt before — lightheaded but languorous and sensual. They continued kissing for a while, and then she felt David's hand pushing her skirt up, above her knee. She wanted to stop him, but at the same time she wanted him to find his way into her cotton bloomers, to part her hairy lips with his deft fingers and sink into her wetness. She couldn't believe what was happening, and at the same time she had never felt so free. She and Boyo had been married very young, an arranged marriage, and even before this they had grown up together in the same village, so that he was almost like a brother to her. When they were finally alone together, naked in a bed, as adult man and wife, it was all so natural, so calm and safe. But that had all been ripped apart.

David's hand by now had found its way not only into her bloomers, but right up inside her. He moved his fingers so strongly and so swiftly she was completely taken off guard. She gasped and cried out a little — luckily very few people had decided to attend the four-thirty screening of *Now, Voyager*. David continued with his movements, playing her like an instrument, until she wet all over his hand, her bloomers, the seat. David murmured "Oh god … *yes!*" even though she was mortified by what had happened. This had only occurred a few times with Boyo, and she had gotten up dutifully each time and placed a towel or a rag on the wet spot on the bed, ashamed. She could not believe it had happened *now* with this person, a virtual *stranger* in a *cinema*! David was calmly wiping off his hand with the same handkerchief that he had offered her earlier to wipe her tears with. He now offered it to her again, asking if she wanted to clean up.

After this episode, David began calling on Doree in earnest, but always to carry her out. Beach, picnic at the Botanic Gardens, a walk along the harbour, the cinema and then for ice cream. He always carried his flask, and by now Doree was accustomed to the taste of rum and the happy and sexy way it made her feel. David knew that there were men who would pay for a woman like Doree — clean, sweet, and dumb, with a pretty, childlike face and a figure that, with the right clothes and some fattening up, would attract customers. But her main selling point, David knew, was that sweet nectar he could coax out of her at will. He thought about putting her to work in one of the clubs on the main road, or maybe a bar farther east, maybe Barataria. A friend of his was opening a new joint there. He just had to keep working his charm.

Eventually David carried Doree to a nightclub in the heart of Town. He bought her some party clothes beforehand to show her off. When they arrived at the club, he introduced her to lots of people. She didn't know that David knew so many people. Men and women. Indians and many many Creoles and Chinese people, and Whites (local French Creoles and American servicemen) and mulattos. At first she felt out of place, but after a few drinks (this time David ordered rum punches from the bar for both of them), she was laughing at the jokes one of the men told, and after even more drinks, she felt someone's hand on her thigh. The band struck up a hot number, and someone else whisked her off to dance. And then another someone pulled her into a dark corner, into an even darker room, closed the door, pulled up her dress, pulled down her panties, and raped her.

When he was done, she collapsed to the floor in shock, not quite sure how she had let that happen. She *must* have let that happen. What would David say? Had he seen? She pulled up her panties, straightened her dress, smoothed her hair, and opened the door. She slowly made her way back to the main room of the club, not wanting to draw attention to herself. She saw David with a man at the bar. They were laughing and slapping each other on the back. The man was handing David some money, which David put in his vest pocket. He was smiling.

Later that night, as he dropped Doree off in front of the little board house, David handed her a sheaf of bills. "Here," he said. "This is for you."

•

AUNTY DOREE, AS SHE CAME TO BE KNOWN IN HER LATER years, ran a rum shop for over a decade on the Western Main Road in St. James. By the time she was thirty-five, she had saved up enough money from trading on her nectar to open it. People said she drank as much as she sold, but still no one could say they had seen her fall off one of her own bar stools or pass out in a canal. The same nectar that had trapped her that day in the cinema, nectar produced out of the blood, sweat, and tears of canecutters, was the same nectar that brought forth her own special brand of sweet, tropical nectar, a flowing nectar that made men flock to her like bees to honey. Both these nectars had brought her wealth. But only one nectar eventually made her breath sweet with thrush, her brain foggy and forgetful, her liver bloated and scarred.

Her tombstone read:

> Rum was her lover.
> Rum was her friend.
> Rum was her fortune.
> Rum was her end.
> R.I.P. Aunty Doree 1924–1969.

iii. The sweetness of unrequited love and martyrdom

People said Regla was the most beautiful woman from Grande to Carenage. Her skin was smooth smooth smooth, dark and polished like a nutmeg, and she liked to wear small gold earrings to set it off. She had one gold tooth that also mirrored the richness of her skin, and with her high, full breasts and curvaceous backside, she drew men to her wherever she went. As much as Regla could have advantaged men with all that beauty, she didn't. She attracted men, but once they made advances to her and realized that she was not going to put up a fight, that she was, in fact, wide open, they lost interest. Still, there were those so determined to possess her body that they stuck around long enough to do so, occasionally plying her with trinkets and dinners to assuage their guilty Catholic consciences, believing this was their entrance fee, then ravishing her on top of sodden cotton sheets in the night heat of full moons and dry season copulation.

These men soon wearied of her givingness, her ease, her generosity. These men wanted pursuit, challenge, sparks, the whiff of a horner man perhaps — but Regla gave off none of those vibes. Men especially ran from her cravings for more: more of their time, more of their love, more of their heart. She would be left unsatisfied again and again and again. Too soon the men would smell the wedding ring, the baby and bassinette and nappies, and the lifetime of responsibility she gave off like a funky odour. Her tempting body was now a trap, a trap that might, like a siren, lure them and leave them ruined on its rocks. Each time a man advanced, Regla would unwittingly repel him by reminding him of his mother, who had kept him stiflingly close as a replacement for his father, or a grandmother who had doted on him endlessly, even — or especially — when he was bad, or an aunt who called him doux-doux and sweet boy for no other reason than the fact he existed.

As she matured, Regla longed more and more for the embrace of a child, the weight of carrying an infant first in her belly and then in her arms, of rocking a little one to sleep, the smell of baby breath, the fullness of milk in her breasts. Manuel, the sexy Dougla from Valencia, had come, conquered, and fled, like all the others. But then, surprisingly, he had returned a few months later, and thus began a cycle of moving in and out of her life. Approaching thirty, Regla felt desperate. She had done this dance with Manuel three or four times now, for the better part of a year. Manuel would reappear after a three- or four-month absence; make mad, passionate love to her for a string of weeks, telling her how much he missed her, how she could really make him happy, how he was thinking of settling down now, how they could really be something together; and then shortly after that, the fights would start. She could do nothing right; her cooking was terrible. Why didn't she clean up the house at least? It was a mess! Her laugh was irritating, her nose was too big, she didn't know how to satisfy him in bed like other women. This would all culminate in one massive blowout where he would pack up all of the things he had installed in her home over the few months he had stationed himself there (shirts, pants, toothbrush, shaving lotion, deodorant, briefs) and clear out. Regla would not hear from him for another three to four months, and she would feel very blue, crying and crying while listening to all the tabanca songs on the radio.

In desperation she asked her friend Juanita for some kind of work to tie Manuel to her, at least long enough so that they could have a baby together. Juanita stared at her for few seconds, wondering if her friend had lost her mind. She knew Manuel was shady, that he was just using Regla; she had also heard that Manuel had a string of women up and down the East-West Corridor, and probably a string of children to boot; she had even heard that he was married.

"Regla!" she started in. "*Why* you would want a child wit a snake like Manuel! Look, it have *nice* men all about de place."

She paused. "And god knows you don't ha no tree growing in yuh face!"

But Regla would have none of it; she begged and pleaded with her friend, talking about what a sweet brown pickney she and Manuel could make. So Juanita told Regla to write her and Manuel's names together on a piece of paper, fold up the paper several times ("*Toward* you, not *away* from you!"), and then wrap a whole spool of red thread around it until it became a ball, then put this ball in a bottle of sugar water and hide it away somewhere no one would see.

Regla followed Juanita's instructions and in two twos Manuel was back on her doorstep, this time with a bouquet of red roses. Not only did he bring flowers, but when he carried her into the bedroom, professing that she was the *only* woman he could ever really love, undressed her, positioned himself over her, he did not even pause to put a condom on. Regla noticed all this, but said nothing. While he was inside her, *he* suddenly began talking about how he wanted to give her a child. She couldn't believe it. She didn't know who this new Manuel was, but she responded, "Yes! Yes!" stroking his back and even nibbling his ear a little.

So they were back in the honeymoon stage of their routine. Mad, passionate lovemaking, this time sans condom. Regla was *sure* she would get pregnant. By the third month of their reunion, she had skipped two periods. She said nothing. One month later, Manuel was still sticking around. She finally decided to tell him the news. She had gone to the doctor to confirm.

"Yeah ... I see dat" was all he said, and he went back watching the TV.

Regla was hurt. She expected him to be as excited as she was. In Regla's mind, this was Manuel's first child. In reality, Manuel the sexy Dougla from Valencia had lost count of how much pickney he had. He had started to breed gyal at fourteen. He was now thirty-five. Some of dem chirren he did check for, and the child mother too. But there were some gyal he brush that he never follow up with, so who really knew?

Despite Manuel's disinterest, Regla began preparing for the baby. She took her paycheque and spent most of it at Excellent Stores and Cookies n Cream and Pennywise, buying baby clothes and shoes and diapers and lotion and Vaseline and baby powder and a thermometer and endless baby bottles. Soon after she had broken the news to Manuel, she was walking down Frederick Street one day on her lunch hour and started to feel one set of cramping. Not wanting to take any chances, she decided to call her work and tell them she was taking the rest of the day. But waiting on Broadway for a car to carry her home, the cramping intensified. She was afraid she might be bleeding.

This was the first miscarriage Regla experienced. In all there would be five — three for Manuel (he stuck around long enough to impregnate her two more times, then was jailed on maintenance charges; one of his child mothers had had enough), and then, after Manuel, she miscarried two more times for Johnson, a down-on-his-luck labourer who came to work on her wall and ended up staying for two years. Her womb revolted and spewed out fetus after fetus after fetus. With each loss, her heart broke more and more. She felt she never really recovered from each loss, that she existed in a constant state of grief. By the time she was approaching forty, Johnson was gone, having cleared out her savings and apparently migrated (she had made her bank account joint with him when he told her he wanted to go to trade school and become certified). At the age she was at, she knew she would probably never hold her own child.

In an effort to find something to do with her hands, Regla took up baking. At first it was just a hobby, but she found that, being alone, she ended up eating most of what she baked. She put on fifty pounds in one year, and her blood sugar went dangerously high. So she decided she would bake to sell. Currants roll, coconut

drops, sponge cake, wedding cakes, birthday cakes, black cake for
Christmas, any and all manner of confectionary. She baked for
children's birthdays and christenings. Sometimes she imagined it
was her own lost child that she was baking for, and she would pour
extra love into the batter, the icing, the whole creation. She was
baking birthday cakes for the same children she had baked chris-
tening cakes for. She stood on the sidelines, watching babies born,
children growing, couples pairing off and having more babies. She
was watching others celebrate life, and she provided the sweetness
for them to celebrate their lives with.

Anytime she ran into someone she hadn't seen in a while: "Eh
eh! But yuh put on size!"

She got big. Bigger. Her breath got sweet. By forty-five, she was
almost three hundred pounds and had been diagnosed with diabetes. "Sugar," the doctor had said to her matter-of-factly, watching her over his glasses and assuming by her colour and her size
that she was of a particular class and level of education, the kind
of person that called diabetes *sugar* instead of by its proper medical
name.

Regla found solace in the Catholic Church. She liked to go and
listen to the folk mass, clap her hands and sing, and then pray. She
asked God why she had had to suffer so much. Why all her children had been taken from her. Why even now there was neither
child nor man to comfort her. Sometimes, praying on her knees in
the church, she would cry. Then she would go to the altars for the
saints and light candles for the five children she would never know,
never hold, never get a chance to love.

A day came when the doctor told her she had an infection in
her foot. Sepsis. She had been ignoring the pain, telling herself
it was nothing, furiously baking her confections, never wanting
to disappoint a client, especially a child who was waiting on one
of her specialty cakes. Now the doctor was telling her she would
lose her leg. When she watched him numbly, in shock, he shouted

"Dey go cut off yuh foot!" again, assuming her silence indicated a low level of intellect, the kind of ignorance typical of the masses. This was too much for Regla. After the operation, she felt she had lost the will to live. She thought more and more about who the five children would have been had they lived and grown up. Secretly, after each miscarriage, she had given each lost soul a name, so now she spoke openly to these formless children, her little angels in heaven. She thought that had they lived, they would have taken care of her now, better care than she had taken of herself, and she would also probably still have her leg. And even if she had still gained all the weight, and still fallen ill, at least she would have had the comfort of them around her now as she lay in a hospital bed, a bloody stump where one of her shapely legs had once been.

A year later she lost her other leg. She was now round, fat, black, and legless. "Like a toolum!" she heard one of the nurses say to another while they made their rounds. They howled wildly together, not seeming to care if she heard them or not.

iv. The sweetness of satiation

Newton grew up on the Hill, and from a very young age would wander into the local parlour shop with a few red dollars to buy a sweetie or a biscuit or a sugary sweet drink. Everyone joked about Newton's sweet tooth, how he could be lured to do anything just by dangling something sweet before him. His mother had to work two jobs to try to keep body and soul together, and his older sister was caught up in a turbulent romance with the local bully. He was most often left in the care of Granny, who was fading in and out of dementia. But one thing that Granny could still do was make sweets: sugar cake, a mean pone, condensed milk fudge, toolum, ice cream, and sweet bread. So Newton would plop himself in front of the television with Granny, munching away happily on whatever concoction she had whipped up that day. A Coke in one hand, a piece of pone in the other, Newton was content, watching cartoons and Bollywood movies and whatever else the local station chose to broadcast. By the time his mother got home, exhausted, Newton would have already washed up and gone to bed. When he woke in the morning, his mother would have already left, having to walk quite far down the hill before dawn in the chill of dew, looking for a P car to carry her to work at the chocolate factory. Newton would grab whatever he could find to eat before heading out the door to school. Sometimes it would be a piece of fudge, sometimes a piece of discarded chocolate his mother had brought back from the factory, or maybe a sweet drink. Even though he was only six, Newton was already putting on size. His mother was distressed that he could not fit into the hand-me-downs from his older cousin Benny — Newton was far bigger in girth even though Benny was two years older than him.

Newton was eight when Granny died, and he consoled himself with food, not only the food she used to make, all the sweet things that reminded him of her, but all manner of junk food. By the time he was ten, he had already reached one hundred pounds. He found it difficult to manoeuvre the hill that they lived on, so he would beg his mother for taxi fare so that he would not have to climb up and down the hill twice a day, sweating, red-faced, the other children laughing at him. At school his classmates called him Fat Boy and Tubawumbs. Although he used to laugh it off, inside he didn't feel so good about the name-calling. He took to buying Kiss cakes with his lunch money, and with what was leftover he would purchase a small tub of ice cream and carry it home after school to eat in front of the TV, watching some of the same shows he had watched with his Granny years earlier.

His sister by this time had not only moved out of the family home, but had migrated to Canada. She was working up there in a factory, and sometimes he overheard his mother talking to his sister long distance. He knew that Kaylene was telling his mother how much work there was up there in Toronto, how she could get a job easy easy. Sometimes when he was in the other room, he would overhear his mother say "Gyal, if I could I would — but what about Newton?" He didn't understand why he couldn't go to Canada too. Maybe he would like it up there. One day he overheard his mother say to Kaylene, "I have my visa in order. When you sending the ticket?" He pulled a half-eaten packet of Biskrem biscuits out of his pocket and started munching on them. Were they just going to leave him here? Alone?

The day came when his mother was ready to leave. She was waiting on the car to carry her to the airport, and she reminded Newton that he was a big boy and he could look after the house while she was gone; that her friend Angel would be stopping in to see about him every day and would be dropping off groceries and money for travel; and that old Mr. Toulouse down the road was where he should go if there was any kind of trouble. His aunt Verna was quite in Tobago with his cousins, but she had promised to come to Trinidad for the Easter break, which was only three weeks away, and she and his cousins Benny and Letisha would be coming to stay for a fortnight. His mother said she would call him when she could, and repeated that on the fridge were numbers for police, fire, and disaster management (in case there was an earthquake or anything like that). Newton watched her numbly. She had been a constant absence in his life even though they had been living under the same roof for years. There was a lump in his throat, and he fingered the Catch bar he had stashed in his trouser pocket. She never told him when she would return.

Newton's size shielded him in many ways from what could have happened to a boy his age abandoned by his mother in a not-so-nice neighbourhood. He looked older than he was, and so the fellas on the corner didn't interfere with him too much. He kept to himself, spending his time watching TV, playing on his Game

Boy, and eating sweets. It took a while before people began to inquire after his mother. They really weren't accustomed to seeing her around the neighbourhood anyway, as she always left in the dark and returned in the dark. His birthday came and went; his mother called him periodically. Angel came every couple of days and dropped off groceries for him and money, which he used to buy KFC and snacks and not much else. Newton felt nothing. He numbed his feelings with food. His only sensation was the rush he felt with sugar.

He regularly fell asleep in class. His teacher, violently shaking him, was angry, the other students joyous. "Wha'appen, fat boy, you was jockin whole night ah wha?" said Larry the class clown.

Newton straightened up in his seat, but the teacher sent him to the principal's office anyway. The principal sighed and said, "You again? What it is? Every afternoon yuh feel is to nap een school?"

Newton sat across from the principal. He knew that after lunch he only felt to knock out. Like sugar, sleep was a blissful escape. Anaesthetized, he didn't have to feel, or think about, anything.

The car dropped him up the hill as usual after school. He noticed Mr. Toulouse watering his plants in his yard.

"Newton, how you going?"

Since his mother had left, he had had no cause to go by Mr. Toulouse. Nothing dangerous or frightening had happened. He had just kept to himself. But he knew Mr. Toulouse was aware of his situation, so he responded, "Ah dey."

Like Newton, Mr. Toulouse was a big person. He lived alone. No one had ever seen anyone come in or out of Mr. Toulouse's house except for Mr. Toulouse and workmen who came from time to time to do repairs.

"Yuh mudder back as yet?"

"No." Newton was sweating in the late afternoon sun. He wanted to change out of his school clothes, bathe, and eat sweets in front of the TV, his usual routine.

"Yuh like chocolate?"

Newton was confused. "Yes?" he said.

"Right. Well, ah now bake a chocolate cake. Ah does bake, yuh know!" Mr. Toulouse smiled, a big toothy grin. "Why don't you come and get a piece? Ah cyan eat all mehself — look at me!" He chuckled.

Newton was not one to turn down homemade chocolate cake. He couldn't remember the last time he had tasted a piece of home-made cake. Homemade, like his Granny used to bake. "Oright."

Mr. Toulouse ushered him into his yard and then into his house. The blinds were all drawn and Mr. Toulouse had the air conditioning up high. He had a fifty-eight-inch big-screen tele-vision and surround sound. There was a cooking show on. Newton was mesmerized.

"Siddown, siddown. Ah go bring de cake."

Newton sat down on a comfortable plush sofa. The White people's heads on the television screen were life-size. They were basting some lamb in apricot and honey sauce.

"Here you go." Mr. Toulouse handed Newton a generous piece of double-layered, iced chocolate cake with chocolate curls and mocha dusting. Newton's eyes lit up. He took the plate, fork, and napkin Mr. Toulouse handed him. Mr. Toulouse sat next to him on the sofa.

Newton took a bite of the cake. It was like nothing he had ever tasted. It was light and fluffy, and the whipped frosting had a hint of espresso and orange in it. It literally melted in his mouth.

"Yuh like de cake?" Mr. Toulouse smiled at him widely, and put his hand on Newton's knee.

Newton watched the hand, and took another bite of the cake.

v. The sweetness of oblivion

Jack had a good life. He had a good job with the government, in the tax division, and this allowed him to afford the nice four-bedroom house in a nice suburban enclave not too far from Town. His pretty wife also had a career — she worked as an administrator in the health-care system — and their two children were both doing well in school. But one day Jack fell down — *boops!* — at work. His co-workers rushed to his aid. Are you all right? Should we call an ambulance? But Jack shook it off. He felt fine. Until it happened again. And again. Then one day, he fell down at home. Jack had a grand mal seizure in front of his children. He peed and shit himself. His wife, having seen these types of seizures before in her profession, knew what to do. She ended up calling the ambulance, and Jack was admitted to hospital for observation and a series of tests.

Inconclusive.

Jack tried to go back to work and act like everything was normal, but he was very worried. His wife, too, would lay awake at night, wondering what they were going to do. It got to the point where Jack had to take a sick leave from his work because his "spells" were increasing in frequency. The doctors in Trinidad suspected he might have a form of multiple sclerosis, but they weren't certain. There was talk of Lyme disease. They started giving him a cocktail of drugs, hoping that somehow this roulette would achieve a perfect storm of success in Jack's body. For a while it looked like he might be improving, but then the seizures would start up again. He was hospitalized a second time.

Jack had a family member in Miami. The family member offered to assist with medical bills so that Jack could come up to the States and get properly tested. He went, hopeful. At the end of it, finally, a diagnosis. Neurosarcoidosis.

The prognosis was grim. Incurable. They could try to manage symptoms with drugs, but these drugs came with a lot of side effects. Jack went back to Trinidad, depressed. He had told his wife the news over the phone, but he didn't know how to tell his children. They were so young.

Once he was back home, he began to Google everything he could find on neurosarcoidosis.

> Symptoms may include:
> Delirium
> Vertigo
> Confusion
> Hearing loss
> Dementia
> Vision problems
> Loss of sight
> Loss of taste and smell
> Seizures
> Fatigue

His heart sank. He clicked on Treatment.

No cure. Medication to reduce the inflammation in the brain. Some studies had shown diet could play a factor. Sugar had been known to trigger symptoms.

He shared this information with his wife. She went through the house, meticulously ridding it of all sugar. Demerara, refined, icing, golden, cubed. Cookies, pastries, waffles, donuts, biscuits, chocolate, cereals were next. Ice cream — tossed. Hard candies in a bowl — eliminated. Syrup, jams, spreads, honey — trashed.

It was hard at first to live without sugar. The kids were especially upset, but Jack's wife made sure to take them out to Häagen-Dazs at least once a week for a treat, without Jack knowing. She told them Daddy was on a diet so he couldn't eat sugar and they were not to let him know that *they* had eaten some!

Months passed. No episodes. Jack returned to work.

The next seizure that Jack had lasted for three days. He couldn't speak or recognize anyone afterward. He was in diapers and restraints. His wife began to let close family know, in case they wanted to say their goodbyes. No one knew what was going to happen next. Weeks later, Jack was back at home, convalescing. He had regained some of his faculties. He knew who everyone was, and he had recouped speech, but he could not recollect his time in the hospital.

One evening after dinner, Jack's wife found him rummaging in the freezer.

"Where is the ice cream?"

"We don't have any. Remember, we got rid of it when we learned sugar is bad for you?"

"I want ice cream!"

"Well, we don't have any."

"*WHAT DE FUCK IS THIS? I can't have any ice cream in my own fucking house?*"

Jack grabbed the car keys from the table. Before his wife could stop him he was in the driveway, getting into his car.

"You can't drive! You just came out of hospital!"

Jack slammed the door viciously in his wife's face and peeled out of the driveway. He did not come back for two hours.

And so it began. No matter what Jack's wife did — plead, beg, cry, scream, cuss, shout — Jack was determined to eat ice cream. And cookies. And chocolates. He craved sugar more than anything. She took to hiding his car keys. He took to recruiting people to bring him his fix. Even his children pleaded with him to stop eating sugar. He told them they were scornful, hideous little brats and should never have been born.

One night Jack's wife woke up in the middle of the night to see that Jack was not in the bed. She feared the worst. Not in the bathroom. Not at the bottom of the stairs. Where was he?

She found him naked outside in the driveway, wielding a cutlass, slashing the night air as if he were cutting cane.

Acknowledgements

To all my beloved Eguns, without whose sacrifices I would not be here today.

To the team at Dundurn Press, whose feedback was invaluable and whose support was graciously welcomed.

To my husband J., who gave me the space to write and who really listened.

To our wonderful dogs — the Rotts and Rescues crew — who keep me company, interrupt me constantly, and have my back always.

And finally: Maferefun Ellegua Laroye, Maferefun Ochún Ibu Kole – pa'siempre.

About the Author

 Camille Hernández-Ramdwar is a multiracial, multicultural, multilingual, and transnational writer, scholar, and consultant. She began writing as a child and had her first poems published as a teen. In her twenties her work appeared in numerous anthologies and journals; she was then sucked into the vortex of academia as a means of raising her family and paying the bills. After many years toiling in academia, she is thrilled to return to creative pursuits. The veil between the corporeal and the incorporeal is very thin in her work, which explores the search for belonging; the collective violences of neo-colonialism, poverty, racism, sexism, and other injustices; and the important interrelationship between matter and spirit. Camille divides her time between Toronto and Trinidad and Tobago, where when she is not writing, she is tending to dogs, plants, and the unseen powers.